CAJUN KIDS ADVENTURES

VOLUME ONE

MYSTERY
AT
INDIAN POINT

CAJUN KIDS ADVENTURES

VOLUME ONE

MYSTERY

AT

INDIAN POINT

C. P. LANDRY

EXCALIBER PUBLISHING SERVICES, INC.

CAJUN KIDS ADVENTURES- VOLUME ONE

MYSTERY AT INDIAN POINT

Copyright © 2022 by C. P. Landry. All rights reserved.

Published by Excaliber Publishing Services, Inc.

P.O. Box 280, Maurice, Louisiana   70555

info@excaliberpublishing.com

Cover illustration by Steve Shamburger.   www.steveshamburger.com

Interior illustrations by Camryn L. Landry and Steve Shamburger

Book design and layout by Cajun Kids Adventures, LLC.

Published in the United States of America

ISBN: 979-8-9856399-0-2

Library of Congress Control Number: 2022909029

Louisiana

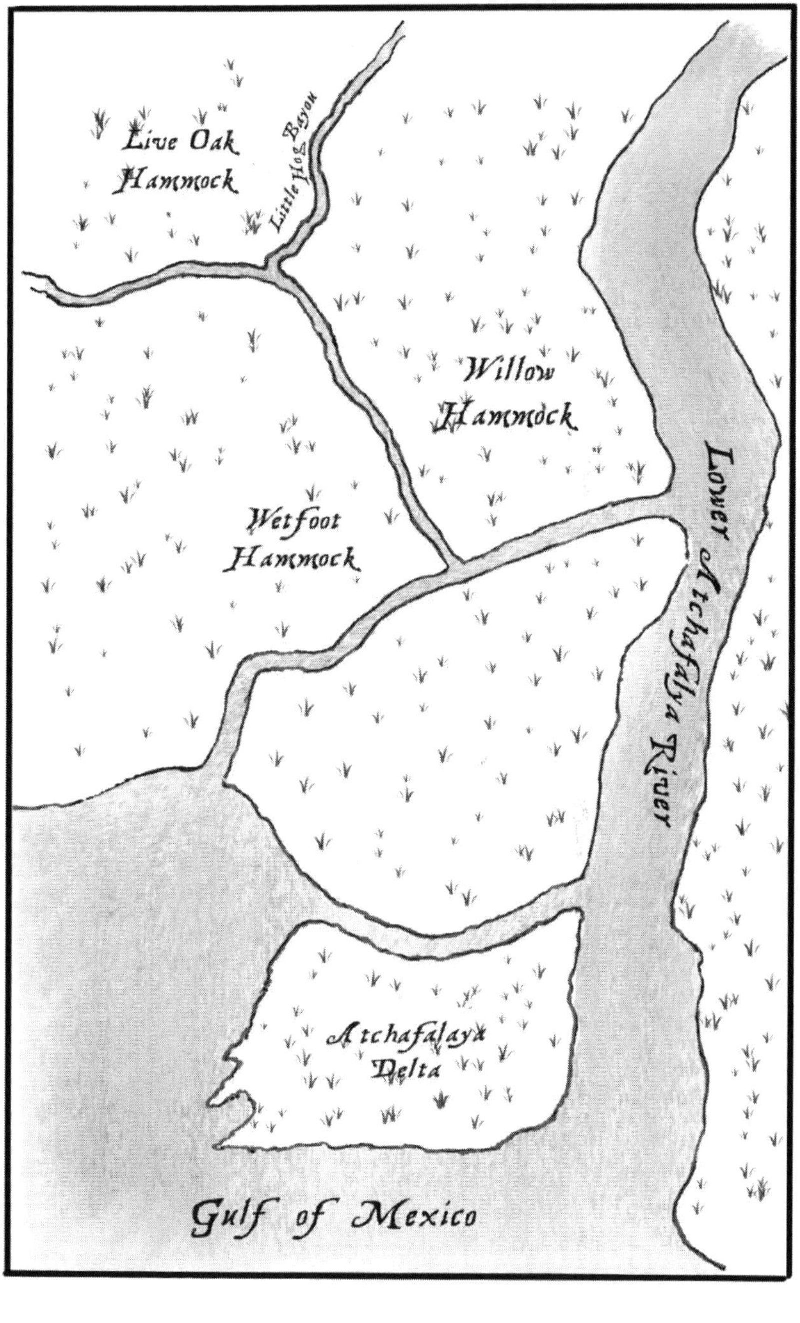

Live Oak
Hammock
Little Hog Bayou
Willow
Hammock
Wetfoot
Hammock
Lower Atchafalaya River
Atchafalaya
Delta
Gulf of Mexico

Words to be Familiar With

airboat – Flat-bottom boat driven by an airplane propeller and controlled by large rudders in the rear of the boat.

bayou – A small river or creek. Mostly used in the southern U. S.

cistern – A tank that is used for storing rainwater.

gumbo – A thick soup or stew made with seafood or chicken, mainly cooked in the southern United States, especially in Louisiana.

hammock – Wooded area or ridge that rises above the marsh.

houseboat – A large flat-bottomed boat or barge equipped to be used as a home.

marsh – Low-lying area of land that is covered by water. Mostly covered with tall grasses and void of trees.

pier – A platform built over the water used to secure boats.

reef – Ridge of sand, rock or coral near the surface of the water.

swamp – Low-lying wooded land that is covered by water.

tide – The rise and fall of the planet's water surface, caused by the gravitational pull of the moon and sun.

wharf – A structure built alongside a waterway used to secure boats.

The Houseboat at

Willow Hammock

CHAPTER ONE

A light fog on the water slowly faded away as rays of sunlight crept over the treetops. It had been cooler the last couple of mornings than it was earlier in the week. The first cold weather to hit the bayous of South Louisiana usually didn't come until late October, but this year it made an earlier and much-welcomed appearance. The cooler temperatures meant the change of seasons was drawing near, and the effects it would have on the surroundings were almost magical.

The lush, thick greenery that lined the banks of the rivers and bayous would soon transform into hues of orange and red. Alligators and turtles basking in the sun would begin to nest for the winter, ushering in ducks and other waterfowl returning to enjoy the mild gulf coast weather. The early morning cry of seagulls feeding along the waterways would be replaced by the distant echoes of geese honking. As the leaves fell and

1

the marsh began to turn brown and thin out, wildlife which once seemed invisible would appear almost everywhere.

The changing sights and sounds helped to make autumn a beautiful experience. But the one thing that always seemed to stand out most at this time of year was the laughter that could be heard up and down the bayous. That wonderful sound was created by five young children growing up in a little piece of paradise in the swamps and marshes of South Louisiana known as Willow Hammock.

It started out a typical morning at Willow Hammock. The children woke at dawn to start their schoolwork, with hopes of finishing early enough to have the afternoon off. They knew the light wind that blew from the north would push the tide a little lower than normal. And a lower tide meant more riverbank to be explored.

Elizabeth Ann, or Beth as she liked to be called, was the oldest of the five children. At the age of fourteen, she was tall and slender, with a tanned complexion and long blonde hair. She had been working on a chart of high and low tides as part of her science project on weather for the past several weeks. Confident in her work, she knew that the low tide created by the water being pulled into the Gulf of Mexico was going to be between two o'clock and three o'clock in the afternoon. Finishing her schoolwork to have the entire afternoon to take an outing with her brothers and sister would not be a problem.

Mark David, aware of Beth's plan, had no doubt he would be joining his sister to explore the sandy riverbanks. At the age of thirteen, he was a husky, strong lad whose curiosity and thirst for knowledge had formed an adventurer and inventor not afraid to try anything. Although considered somewhat of a bookworm, he'd proven himself to be quite handy to have around when trouble arose.

The decision to homeschool because of his father's job as a land manager was a blessing for Mark. He loved rising early in the morning to begin his studies, which meant he could have most of his schoolwork done long before the others. This meant more time to work on his projects and inventions. Mark could fix or make almost anything. It was not unusual to find him headfirst in his father's trash bin at the workshop, picking through scrap wood, wire, rope, old motors and other things. His father would chuckle about how many times he could throw the same thing away. But Mark had one belief when it came to a good pile of junk, "One man's trash is another man's treasure."

But the treasure that would soon appear along the banks of the river as the water crept lower was his focus now. Finishing his schoolwork on time was not a worry. In fact, Mark planned to have his backpack loaded with walking sticks and a shovel ready for when the others walked out the door.

Right when he thought nothing could go wrong with their plan, Mark suddenly heard a sound coming from the other side of the room. If he had to describe the sound, it somewhat resembled his Uncle Gus's hound dog moaning in its sleep.

Curious, he peered over his shoulder. The sound came from his brother Timmy, sitting with his pencil in hand and a blank look on his face. That was the look that appeared quite often when the young boy's brain slipped into overload.

Timothy Red, the middle child of the five siblings, was a spirited young boy of ten years old. Freckle-faced with a lanky build, he had the ability to bring any room to life with his antics and flair for dramatics.

Timmy was also a true outdoorsman, which could have been why he was having trouble focusing on his schoolwork this morning. "It is such a beautiful day to be locked inside," he thought to himself. A short time before his moaning, he watched a Kingfisher land on a tree limb just outside the window. As it fluffed its feathers and groomed itself, Timmy's mind began to wander.

He had no idea how long he had been staring out the window when his mother came by and tapped him on the shoulder. It was shortly after that he let out the moan, realizing that he completely lost his train of thought.

His mom, who watched the whole event from the kitchen table, quickly moved in for the rescue. She had been down this road before and knew how to handle it. Very calmly, she told him to take out his science book, explaining to him that he would have to plan on finishing his math sheet later. Timmy liked science, especially the chapters about reptiles that they were studying now. He peeked over his shoulder for a second to see Beth and Mark looking back at him with concern. He smiled at them and raised one eyebrow in a way that only he could do, letting them know he was not going to let them down. The plan would not change because of him.

His mother, relieved to see him reading and answering his worksheet, realized early in their homeschool days that each child required something different to bring out their best. For Timmy, keeping things interesting helped to keep his attention. She learned math and word games that kept the young boy focused on his studies while still enjoying them. She also learned that closing the window blinds definitely kept Timmy out of trouble. A bug crawling across the window screen, a bird flying by, or even a gust of wind causing the trees to sway could catch his attention. And when that happened, Timmy's brain would completely go blank. So, it became his mother's job to try everything possible to keep his attention on schoolwork while at his desk. And living at a place like Willow Hammock, where adventure and excitement always waited right around the corner, made that job very difficult at times. But for his mother, the extra work was worth it.

She enjoyed living away from the city, or "down the bayou," as the locals called it. It was a peaceful life on the houseboat at Willow Hammock. Leaving the life of cell phones and internet was challenging at first, but it was something she was starting to enjoy. Although there was cell phone reception if someone chose to climb to the roof of the generator shed, she made an easy choice to just leave her phone turned off. The occasional trips to the library while in town for supplies became the older children's opportunity to do research with their laptops and gather information needed to complete their schoolwork. It took very careful planning to make sure the children's schoolwork continued without interruption.

Another luxury of city living unavailable at Willow Hammock was around-the-clock electricity. A generator supplied them with power when it was needed. Every day at dusk, the children's father would start the generator to power the houseboat. It was at that time laundry could be done, electronics could be recharged, and air conditioning was available. In the summer the generator and air conditioner would run throughout the night. But in the winter, when air conditioning was not needed, the generator would be turned off at bedtime. The children's mother cherished those nights. With the windows lifted, the sounds of the wildlife scattered throughout the bayous and marshes could be heard for miles. Great Horned Owls calling to each other in the distance and coyotes howling at the moon pierced the silence of the night. Bobcats screamed in the darkness, letting the other creatures of the night know that this was their territory. The sounds that echoed through the waterways during the night stirred so many childhood memories for the children's mother.

Water usage was another thing that was constantly monitored. At Willow Hammock, there was no such thing as a long shower. Rainwater captured from the roofs of the houseboat and generator shed dumped into large water tanks called 'cisterns.' All of the water used for cooking, cleaning and showering came from the cisterns. For that reason, keeping safe, clean water became a constant priority.

The children's mother grew up spending her summers and occasional weekends at Willow Hammock with her grandparents. It was a time of great fun and adventure, and she was grateful that her children would now also have a chance to experience the life she remembered.

Her grandparents were the last of the generations to live on her family's land. When her grandfather could no longer fish and trap the land of his ancestors, they were forced to move to town where they could be near family. No one had made Willow Hammock their home since then. And after skipping a generation, she was proud to once again call it 'home.'

There were times, however, when leaving Willow Hammock did not bother her too much because she loved to travel. Whether it was a vacation or mission trip with the children, she was always eager to go.

The children's mother was startled for just a moment as she heard a door slam and two boisterous young children run by the window in front of her. It was Annie and Sam, the two youngest of the family.

Annie and Sam ran straight to the swing set in the yard. That always seemed to be the first stop for them as they made their way out the door.

Sam would usually run headfirst between the chains of the swing, letting the seat grab him in the stomach and just swing there with his legs lifted.

Samuel Carson was a delightful young boy, with bleached blonde hair, a cute round face and rosy cheeks. There was not a bug, lizard, frog or any other critter that could go by without catching his attention. About the only thing that could keep him away from critter hunting was to tag along on an adventure with his brothers and sisters.

"He is all boy," his mother liked to say. Emptying the pockets of his pants each night before doing laundry made his mother very nervous. Finding a frog or dead bug seemed to happen quite often. But she was pretty easy-going when it did happen, and usually got a good laugh out of it.

Ann Marie, or Annie, as she was called, joined her brother at the swing set. She was eight years old, a year older than her younger brother Sam. A beautiful girl with long silky hair and blue eyes, she was much more independent than the other children and always very eager to learn. And for such a quiet and shy young girl, she had a laugh that could be heard a mile away. She also loved the outdoors. Annie knew that on a beautiful day like today something good was going to be planned with her brothers and sister. But for now, she knew that she and Sam would have to wait contently until the others finished their schoolwork.

The children loved to explore the areas around Willow Hammock. There was always something exciting waiting for them. They also knew much of the history of the land, since their mother's family had been living there for several generations.

Their mother's great, great grandfather moved there to be close to the mouth of the Atchafalaya River when he was a young man. At that time, the river was becoming an important route for shipping and trade. He helped build and operate the first lighthouse that guided sailors through the maze of shallow reefs along the river's edge. He raised his family at Willow Hammock, which was located only a few miles north of the lighthouse. When he was not working as a lighthouse keeper, he would fish the waters of their area and sell his catch in town.

In those days, it was a hard life living in the swamps and marshes away from town. There were no motor boats, so a trip to town usually took the better part of a day rowing a boat, or skiff, as they were called in that region, up river. Trips to town for supplies were usually only made once a month. Most of the families who lived south of town along the bayous and rivers learned to live off the land. Small orchards provided fresh fruit and seasonal gardens were a source of vegetables and herbs. Fish and other seafood provided their main source of meat.

By the late 1930s, the postal service began to deliver mail by boat. This created a way for the families along the river to receive supplies from town. Needed medicines and even an occasional doctor's visit were now available. The local merchants in town were able to send groceries and other supplies using the mail boat as their delivery system.

The weekly mail boat also provided something else that was very important: news and information. Newspapers were able to keep the families who lived along the coast up to date on events, approaching storms and severe weather.

The postal service continued delivering mail by boat until the middle of the 1950s. By then, the outboard motor became popular among the people who lived along the waterways. The trip to town that once took most of the day now took an hour or two.

This new source of travel also changed the lives of the people who fished and trapped along the river. They were now able to move to town and return each day to their land to catch their harvest. Homesteads became weekend camps and getaways for the families that once struggled to survive in the harsh areas. By 1970, there were very few people who still were able to call the coastal regions of the mighty river 'home.'

The few that did stay did so for many reasons. But the one thing they all had in common was avoiding the fast-paced life that came with living in town. Life away from town kept things simple for them and that was the way they liked it. Most of them still trapped in the winter and fished in the spring and summer.

But there was one family that did the opposite of those who fled the marshes and swamps to have the luxuries of living in town. It was a family that made the decision to embrace a simpler way of life and call Willow Hammock home.

CHAPTER TWO

"It's only ten minutes after two. We'll have plenty of time to look around," said Beth, as they made their way along the riverbank.

The chill that the north wind brought earlier in the day had now warmed, giving the children a perfect day to go exploring. The destination today was the huge sand bar where the waterway that ran through Willow Hammock met with the Lower Atchafalaya River, which was exposed because of the unusually low tide.

Mark had taken the lead today. He enjoyed clearing the way for the others or finding obstacles they would have to detour around. He also was under the impression that being first meant finding the best treasure, or junk, depending on how you looked at it.

Beth knew better than that. She quite often watched her brothers walk right over unusual rocks, shells and even once an old coin in their haste to be in the front. With her youngest brother Sam at her side, she would carefully scan the bank from one side to the other, stopping often to dig with her finger in the wet sand or to poke around with her walking stick.

Timmy and Annie had no care as to where they were in line. Being out on an adventure was all that mattered to them. Skipping clamshells across the calm water occupied their time today. Annie's laugh could be heard echoing across the riverbanks, being brought on by the never-ending antics of her brother Timmy.

"Mark, you need to slow down a little," Beth yelled, as she looked back over her shoulder to see how far they'd traveled.

Although the point at which the rivers met was only a little over a mile away from the houseboat, it seemed a great distance to the children. From the houseboat, their mother could see them the entire way to the point if they stayed along the riverbank. And Beth knew she was watching. The children had been exploring the banks of the rivers and bayous for as long as they could remember. Their mother and father taught them how to watch for things out of the ordinary and dangerous situations. Although Beth was only fourteen years of age, her mother and father had a great deal of confidence in her ability to care for the other children. And fortunately, her brothers and sister had the same confidence in her.

Being the oldest of five, she was called upon from time to time to take responsibility for activities with the other children and for household duties. Beth was very quick to learn, however, that with responsibility comes reward. She knew that she was fortunate to have the many freedoms that the others were not privileged to. And because of that, she welcomed the challenge.

As they arrived at their destination, the children were pleasantly surprised to find the water lower than expected. The shallow reef that held back the water on normal days now extended over a hundred feet from the water's edge. A second smaller reef, which they had never seen before, wrapped around the point and met up with the larger reef near a small patch of willow trees.

The children excitedly began searching the new territory that the low tide rewarded them with. The two younger children were eagerly searching for snails and unusual shells, each find being compared to the one before.

Timmy kicked and picked through the driftwood and sticks that had washed up against the inside of the reef. It was his opinion that a boy could never have enough wood to make a good pirate sword. Mark headed for the highest part of the bank. He knew it was where the bulk of the river's bounty would be found. Things that had fallen off of the many boats that traveled the great river would usually end up along the banks. And these were the things that Mark was most interested in.

Beth, however, took much more detail in her searches. Today she chose to start at the river's edge, walking the perimeter and returning a little further in. She would repeat that pattern until it brought her to the large shell reef near the trees. As she was making her second pass, she noticed the edge of something protruding from the sand. She uncovered it and went to the shallow water to clean the unknown object. It appeared to be a piece of pottery. It sparked her curiosity enough that she decided to keep it and study it more when she returned home. Putting the piece of pottery in her backpack, she proceeded with her search.

"Hey guys, come here, quick," Timmy yelled. He was standing near the high ground where the two shell reefs came together. "Come see this, hurry," he said excitedly.

As they gathered together, they began to notice that the two reefs did not actually come together, but came about three feet from each other forming a hard, sandy path that led through a patch of willow trees. Inside the willows appeared to be a small, sandy washout surrounded by high banks on all sides.

Making their way through the shaded opening, they could feel a chill in the air and smell the musty, wet trees and earth.

"This must have washed out during the last big storm that hit," Mark said.

He was studying the newly exposed roots of the trees that were sticking out of the mud around the walls of the washout. Mark guessed that it was probably thirty feet from one side of the washout to the other.

"We shouldn't stay in here long. Mom won't be able to see us from the houseboat," Beth told them.

She began looking around to see if there was anything that could be of danger.

"Mark, you need to hold Annie's hand while we are in here, and I'll hold Sam's. Timmy, you need to keep watch for snakes and other things," she said with caution.

"I'm the man for the job," said Timmy, making a quick salute to his sister.

He glanced over at Annie to see if she was laughing. But with the excitement of the new find, she hadn't even noticed his silliness.

"Look at the neat shell," Sam said.

He was holding his hand out toward Beth with a triangular-shaped shell in his hand. As she took a quick look at the shell, Sam rolled it to the tip of his fingers and pulled his arm back to sling it into the soft mud that surrounded them.

"Wait!" Beth yelled, grabbing his wrist. "Mark, come here, quick," she said, as she removed the shell from her brother's hand. "Is this what I think it is?" Beth asked.

Mark's eyes lit up as he studied the object in Beth's hand.

"That's exactly like the Indian arrowheads we saw at the museum we visited last year."

"That's cool," Timmy said, as he made his way over to examine the arrowhead.

Sam drew close to his sister. "Are there Indians around here?" he asked nervously.

"No, silly," Beth replied. "This is probably two hundred years old or maybe even older."

"Let's look around a little longer before we have to go," Mark said.

Just a short time later the silence was broken by Timmy.

"Guys, you have to come see this."

He knelt near the rear of the washout and was picking chunks of mud and sand from around a large object.

Beth asked Mark to take Sam's hand. Then she knelt beside her brother and began carefully digging.

As they continued to dig, the object began to take shape.

"Mark, give me a bottle of water out of your backpack," Beth said.

Beth began pouring water down the sides of the pear-shaped object. She heard gasps behind her as the running water revealed a crude drawing of a hunter throwing a spear at a running deer. Above the drawing, a piece of the upper edge of the object was missing.

"It's Native American Indian pottery," said Mark.

Beth pulled out the piece of pottery she found at the sand bar and placed it on top of the piece in the mud. It was a perfect fit.

"And from the looks of it," Beth said, "this one and any others like it will soon be washed away."

A concerned look came over their faces as they stood and stared at the half-exposed clay vase sticking out of the mud and sand.

"Look to your left, a few feet away," Mark told Beth, "It looks like the edge of another one."

Beth reached over and pulled the sand from around the top of the object.

"It is another one!" she exclaimed, continuing to pull more sand from around the artifact.

"What should we do?" Annie asked.

"Let's keep looking around," Beth answered, "but try not to disturb anything."

The children began searching the washout. In just a short amount of time, they discovered a number of stones that appeared to be tools of some type and also several arrowheads.

"This is amazing," Mark told the others.

"Why do you think this stuff is here?" Annie asked.

"Maybe it is the site of an old village," Timmy replied.

"I don't think so," Beth told him. "There would be no reason for them to bury whole vases and perfectly good tools. This must be some type of sacred site or ceremonial site."

"Why wouldn't we know about this?" Mark asked. "Mom's family has been here for several generations, and it seems like someone would have some type of information about a sacred site."

"The Native Americans that lived in this area could have been gone long before our ancestors arrived," Beth replied.

"You are probably right," Mark said, nodding his head. "I remember Mom saying that her great, great grandfather moved here to help build and maintain the first lighthouse. That would have put him here sometimes around the late 1800s."

"That's right," Beth remarked, "so, Mom's family would have probably never seen any evidence of their existence."

The children continued to explore the washout.

"What are we going to do now?" Timmy asked. "Don't we have to let someone know what we've found?"

"I'm not sure, but right now we need to get back to the riverbank before mom comes looking for us," Mark said. "We've been in here for a long time."

Everyone began to make their way out of the washout. Just as they were reaching the narrow opening that led to the shell reef, they were startled by the thrashing of tall grass and small branches breaking in the distance.

"What is that?" Annie asked with concern.

"I don't know. Whatever it is, it is big and in a hurry!" Timmy shouted.

"Hurry, everybody get to the sandbar!" Mark yelled.

As they emerged from the musty washout onto the sandbar, they heard the distinct sound of high pitch yelping and growling. It was a sound they had all heard before.

"Coyotes!" Timmy yelled.

CHAPTER THREE

"Get out to the riverbank," Mark said, trying to remain calm.

The sunlight caused them to squint their eyes as they rushed out of the dark washout. The yelping of the coyotes began to get closer.

"That tree over there, quick!" Beth yelled, as she grabbed the hands of her youngest brother and sister and ran toward a large willow tree.

The base of the tree split about five feet up from the ground and made a great climbing tree.

"Mark, help me get Sam and Annie up," Beth yelled.

Timmy took a position about ten feet from the tree. He knew that he could climb the tree in just a few seconds if need be, so he decided to hold his ground until the last moment.

Suddenly they heard small limbs breaking and out of the tall grass, just up from the high side of the reef, a deer being followed by a spotted fawn came running out.

"The coyotes are after that deer and her baby," Mark shouted, as he began climbing the tree.

The two deer were crossing in front of the children less than a hundred feet away, when out of the grass came three coyotes.

With Beth, Annie and Sam a safe distance up the tree, Mark yelled for Timmy to start climbing. When he glanced back to see where Timmy was, he noticed that his younger brother had not taken a step.

"Come on, Timmy, now!" yelled Mark.

But instead of Timmy making a run for the tree, he saw him bend over and pick up a rock the size of a tennis ball.

"Timmy, don't you even think about it...."

That was all Mark could get out of his mouth before Timmy took a couple quick steps forward and hurled the rock at the lead coyote.

"You leave those deer alone!" Timmy yelled.

Timmy had always been very athletic. And when it came to throwing, that boy had an arm like a major-league pitcher.

The rock hit the coyote in the side just behind its front leg. The impact of the rock caused the coyote to stumble, rolling head over heels before it turned and ran off into the woods, yelping and whining as it ran. The rock caught the coyote off guard, scaring it more than hurting it.

The two remaining coyotes turned to follow the lead of the first and then froze in their tracks. They turned around slowly and set their eyes on Timmy. The young boy, still holding his walking stick in his left hand, bent down slowly. Without taking his eyes off of the coyotes, he scooped up another large rock in his right hand.

Mark knew what Timmy was about to do and quickly jumped from the tree, landing just a few feet away from his brother. He picked up his walking stick that was lying on the ground. Mark's sudden appearance startled the two coyotes, as they began to pace back and forth nervously.

"Ready when you are," Mark said, with a slight shake in his voice.

"Now!" Timmy yelled as the two boys broke into a run toward the coyotes, screaming and howling as loud as they could.

Timmy released the rock that was in his hand, which hit the ground right in front of the coyotes. The two coyotes jumped and yelped, surprised at the rock. Just then, Mark and Timmy threw their walking sticks like spears at the coyotes. One passed just over the coyotes sticking into the mud. The second spear bounced off the ground and slid under the feet of the coyotes, making them jump to avoid being hit.

The frightened coyotes quickly turned away and, with their tails between their legs, ran into the trees in the same direction as the first one.

Timmy had already picked up another rock and thrown it at the animals before they reached the tall grass at the edge of the trees. Mark quit yelling as soon as the coyotes began their retreat. He hurriedly ran back to the tree to check on his other siblings. He was worried the incident may have frightened the younger children.

Timmy, however, still caught up in the moment, continued yelling while throwing things into the trees.

Beth had heard enough of her brother's noise-making. Swinging down out of the tree, she was yelling before her feet hit the ground.

"Timothy Red, if you don't stop that howling, I'm going to start throwing rocks at you."

Timmy turned and smiled at her.

"Sorry, Sister," he said with a wide grin on his face.

"Guys, we have to get moving," Mark told them, while helping Annie and Sam down from the tree.

As the children began to walk along the riverbank, Annie and Sam quickly joined their brother Timmy.

"Were you scared?" Sam asked.

"Scared, are you kidding me?" said Timmy. "Man, did you see me pop that coyote with that rock? He didn't know what hit him!"

Annie quickly jumped into the conversation.

"If Beth would not have made me climb that tree, I bet I could have popped that coyote too."

"And I could have popped it also," Sam said.

Beth was walking just behind the children with Mark at her side.

"I get the feeling we are going to have to listen to this the whole way home," she said.

"I think you're right," said Mark, as they burst into laughter.

By the time they reach the houseboat, however, the excitement of finding the artifacts almost caused them to forget about the coyotes. They couldn't wait to share with their parents the great discovery they had made that day.

Nearing the houseboat, they heard an airboat approaching from the opposite direction.

"It's Dad!" Annie yelled.

Their father had just stepped onto the wharf and was attempting to tie up his boat when he was attacked by the five children.

"Whoa, whoa, slow down," he said, as all five children were excitedly talking at the same time. "One at a time."

"We found real Native American Indian stuff!" said Annie.

Timmy chimed in next.

"It was so cool. Beth has an arrowhead. Show him," he said moving to the side to let his sister get closer.

"That last storm must have washed out a section of the point," she said holding her hand out for her father to see the arrowhead. "There are also some large vases with drawings on them buried in the mud."

"This is definitely interesting," their father replied, eyeing the arrowhead.

"And we got into a fight with some coyotes," Sam added.

Their father quickly turned his attention from the arrowhead to the children.

"He's exaggerating a little bit," Mark said.

He looked at Mark with concern.

"He better be exaggerating a whole bunch. Now go get cleaned up. I want to hear all about this at supper," their father told them.

The level of excitement was still high at the supper table that night. The children told every detail of their adventure that day. Their father was very interested in the coyote incident.

After hearing the story two times, told once by Beth and the other by Mark, he allowed Timmy to tell why he chose to throw the rock at the coyotes.

"When I saw that fawn running behind her mother," he started, "I had to do something. Throwing the rock was the first thing that came to my mind. And when the other two did not come any closer after seeing us, I figured they didn't know what to do."

"Well first," his father said, "I want to commend you for wanting to help that fawn. That was very brave."

Then he turned to Mark.

"And that was also very brave of you to help your brother."

Their father sat there for a moment, looking at all of the children.

"I'm not saying what you did today was either right or wrong. Every situation is different. Had any of you been alone, I would have expected you to climb that tree and remain perfectly quiet until the coyotes were long gone. And if there would have been a larger group of them, I would've expected you to do the same thing. You must remember that their strength is in numbers. Don't ever forget that. We can coexist with any creature that God has created as long as we have respect for it. Understood?" he asked.

"Yes, sir," they all said together.

"Do you think it's safe for them to go back?" their mother asked.

"I believe so," their father replied. "It's very unusual for coyotes to come that far out to the point. There's not enough cover to keep them concealed. They must have trailed those deer a long way. But just to be safe," he added, "I will take the airboat out there in the morning before I start making my rounds to make sure they headed back to where they came from."

"That would make me feel a whole lot better," their mother said.

The children were all happy to hear that.

Mark quickly responded, "Dad, do you think you and Mom could come to the point tomorrow?"

"I don't see why not. I'll be working out by the northwest property boundary most of the day. I'll just make it a point to be back early enough to go out there."

"Do you think we'll see any Indians?" Sam asked.

"Those Native American Indian tribes moved on a long, long time ago," his father answered.

"What else do you think we'll find?" Beth inquired.

"I have no idea," their father said, "this is something I was not expecting to find at Willow Hammock."

"I have heard lots of stories about the lighthouse keepers and their families that lived around the area with my ancestors, but I have never heard of American Indian tribes that lived close by," their mother added.

"I remember when we first started coming out here years ago, old Mr. Jacobs said that we were going to be surrounded by a lot of history. This may be some of what he was talking about," the children's father told them.

"Dad, we have to go see him," Mark said.

"Okay," their father replied, "you all help your mother clear the table and clean the dishes. I'll see if I can reach Mr. Jacobs on the marine radio. If he's up to it, we will go for a quick visit."

The children cheered with excitement. This was turning out to be a true adventure.

CHAPTER FOUR

Mr. Jacobs' cabin was a fifteen-minute boat ride away. The children loved going there. The old pictures and unusual things that the old trapper found and collected over the years fascinated them.

And of course, there was Bandit, a raccoon that Mr. Jacobs found abandoned as a baby. He cared for the young animal until it was strong enough to survive on its own. But when the time came to release the raccoon into the wild, Bandit wouldn't go. So, the raccoon became a pet. Annie loved Bandit. Whenever they would visit, Mr. Jacobs would give Annie slices of sweet potatoes to feed the raccoon. She would sit there and watch him eat while rubbing the soft fur on the back of his neck. Any chance she could get to visit her furry friend delighted her.

The children could see the lights of Mr. Jacobs' place through the trees before they rounded the bend in the bayou. His cabin was a small, one-room structure elevated five feet above the ground on pilings. The sturdy cabin had withstood many hurricanes and storms over the past sixty years. Mr. Jacobs told them the story a number of times how he built his place when he was just twenty years old. Three generations previously lived on the land that he now hunted, trapped and fished. Many stories of triumph and hardship had been passed down to Mr. Jacobs from his father and grandfather. And there were very few things the children enjoyed more than sitting around the wood-burning stove listening to him tell those stories.

Mr. Jacobs stood waiting on the boat dock as they pulled closer.

"Hello, neighbors," they could hear him yell over the sound of the motor. "Throw me a line," he said to Mark.

As soon as the boat was tied to the dock, the children hurried to greet their friend.

Annie reached Mr. Jacobs first. As he bent over to welcome her, she threw her arms around his neck. Sam, who was only a step behind her, quickly joined in with a big hug.

"There is nothing that brightens my day more than seeing you children," he said while hugging them.

Timmy greeted him next with a hug.

"I whooped some coyotes today," he said.

"That doesn't surprise me," Mr. Jacobs replied, laughing at the boy.

Mark and Beth were the next to come forward to say hello to their friend.

"I just can't imagine what is so important that you would have to come out at this late hour to see an old man like me."

"You are not going to believe what we found," Mark said.

Their mother moved forward between the children to give the old trapper a big hug. She was holding a plate with a large serving of her cherry delight that she baked for their dessert that night.

"Hello, Faith," he said as he hugged her. "We're going to have to make sure we hide that from Bandit, he likes your cooking as much as I do."

"Hello, Mr. Jacobs," the children's father said as he walked up to greet his friend.

"It's always a pleasure to see you, John. Let's go inside, I just put a pot of coffee on."

Mr. Jacobs led the way down the path to the front porch. The constant drone of an old generator could be heard behind the cabin. It powered dimly-lit light bulbs that hung in the trees leading to the cabin.

"When I told Bandit that y'all were coming, he ran straight to the wash basin to get cleaned up. As I was walking out the door to meet you, the last thing I saw was that silly raccoon standing in front of the mirror combing his hair," he said with a wink of his eye.

The children burst into laughter.

"Raccoons don't comb their hair," Annie replied.

The old man began laughing along with them.

As they approached the house, the children could smell smoke from the wood-burning stove.

"Come in and make yourselves at home," Mr. Jacobs said as he held the screen door open for them to pass through.

When they walked through the door of the cozy cabin, the glow of the old wood stove invited them in. Their host lit an oil lamp which sat upon the table in the middle of the room. He did the same to a lamp set atop a chest of drawers next to a bed in the rear corner of the room.

The room seemed to come to life as the light began to cast shadows across the walls and the darkness disappeared. There were paintings hanging on the walls and pictures on the table tops that had been passed from generation to generation. Knickknacks and collectibles, which caught the attention of both young and old, were scattered about the cabin. In the rear corner of the room, opposite the bed, was a small sitting area with an old chair and table. On top of the table sat Mr. Jacobs' family Bible.

Beth had spent countless hours in that old chair flipping through the book. It was filled with pictures and handwritten notes to act as reminders of the events that happened over the years.

In the center of the back wall, another door led to a large back porch. Beyond that, a lighted path led to the outdoor bathroom, or 'outhouse,' as it was called.

Timmy found the outdoor bathroom quite interesting. There was not a visit that went by without the young boy taking a trip to see it. Even after years of watching Timmy stroll out the back door to go to the outhouse, Mr. Jacobs still found it humorous each time it happened.

In the front of the cabin, a small kitchen was set off to one side. The old wood stove burned in the corner with a small pile of firewood stacked alongside. A worn boiling kettle that was set atop the stove appeared to be as old as the stove itself.

On the other side of the cabin, opposite the kitchen, was a work area with a large wooden workbench that ran the entire length of the front wall. That happened to be Mark's favorite part of the house. The old man loved to whittle and carve figures out of wood. The shelves above the bench were filled with small birds and animals, some painted and others not, carved to the smallest detail. Underneath the workbench, pieces of driftwood lay scattered about, waiting to be cut and formed into another treasure in the old trapper's collection.

Soon after Mr. Jacobs lit the lamps, the silence of the room was broken by Sam and Annie greeting Bandit. As he emerged from under the bed, Mr. Jacobs handed the children an old coffee can that held some small pieces of cut sweet potato. The two children sat on the floor giggling and laughing as they fed their furry friend.

The rest of the family sat at the table in the center of the room. Mr. Jacobs poured three cups of coffee and set them on the table along with some sugar and cream.

"I hope you don't mind me eating in front of you," their host said, "this dessert still looks warm."

"Not at all," the children's mother said.

The old man grabbed a fork from the kitchen and sat at the table with the others.

"Now, what is it you wanted to tell me?"

Beth's father nodded to her, prompting her to begin telling the details of their day. Mr. Jacobs listened intently as he ate his dessert.

When Beth finished talking, Mark was able to speak next, filling in small details which seemed important to him. And lastly, Timmy had to tell Mr. Jacobs about the great coyote adventure.

"You children had quite a day," the old man said chuckling.

"The children were hoping you might be able to shed some light about the artifacts they found," their mother said.

"I may be able to help you a little," he said. "When I was a young boy, probably about your age," he said pointing to Mark, "my grandfather used to tell me stories of the Native American tribes that lived in this area. They were friendly for the most part, getting along well with their neighbors. They would trade fresh fish and wild game for flour, salt and other supplies with the merchant ships that traveled up and down the river. My grandfather said that they had also been seen trading their fish and game with the pirate ships that sailed along the coast. He himself once saw a pirate ship anchored in the pass leading to the gulf."

The children sat motionless as he continued.

"The point where you children were this morning, near the eastern tip of your land, was considered sacred to the native tribes. It must have been a burial ground or worship place for them."

"What would you suggest the children do next?" their father asked.

"I would suggest gathering as much information as you can without disturbing anything. Copy the drawings onto a piece of paper and make a list of everything you find. I have a friend I may be able to reach by radio in the morning who could help you."

After they finished talking about the events of the day, the two older children began roaming about the cabin. Their mother and father continued to visit with Mr. Jacobs. Timmy took his trip to the outhouse, as was expected. Thirty minutes later, they were saying their goodbyes as they headed back to the houseboat.

That evening, after the children finished showering and getting ready for bed, they gathered at the table with their father and mother.

"Here's the plan," their father began, "in the morning, I'll take the airboat and run the back side of the ridge on my way out to check the property lines. If everything looks good and I see no signs of coyotes, I'll call your mother on the radio. You can head back out there after you finish your schoolwork. I will swing back by the houseboat as soon as I am done with my work. Your mother and I will take the little boat and head to the point to meet you. How does the tide look tomorrow?" he asked Beth.

"Low tide should be fifteen minutes later than it was today," she replied.

"Perfect," he said, "now everyone hit the sack and get some sleep. You have a big day ahead of you tomorrow."

As they headed to their room, they talked excitedly amongst themselves. Tomorrow could not get here soon enough for them.

****

Mark arose just before daylight the next morning. He woke the others also to make sure they would get an early start. By lunch, they were finishing their full day of schoolwork.

"It's amazing how smooth things can go when you set your mind to it," their mother said with a smile as she put their sandwiches and milk in front of them at the table. "It's a little too early to set out for the point now," she added, "so I would like you to take care of a few chores before you go."

The children looked at her in shock.

Their mother could not help but laugh.

"Your father said he would be here to pick me up about two-thirty. And after that coyote incident yesterday, I do not want you to go too far ahead of us. Understood?"

"Yes, ma'am," they all said together.

It was a few minutes before two o'clock when they set out for the point, having finished the chores their mother gave them. They hurried along the bank, running at times, to reach the opening where the two shell reefs came together.

"Okay," Beth said, "same plan as yesterday. Mark and Annie will stay together, and I will take Sam. Timmy has critter watch."

"After putting a whooping on those coyotes yesterday," Timmy said, "if there is anything out here, it better be watching out for me."

He began hopping around like a boxer, jabbing his fist out in front of him.

"Do you think there is anything out here?" Sam asked nervously.

"It doesn't matter. There ain't nothing I can't whoop," he said, as he continued with his antics.

"If there is anything out here, he's probably already scared it away with his clowning around," Mark said laughing.

"Let's get to work," Beth told them.

Beth and Mark took their pads and pencils out and began making notes.

"Look," Mark said, "one of the vases from yesterday is almost completely exposed."

"And so is the one over here," Beth added.

"The high tide this morning must have washed away more dirt," Mark said.

The children continued exploring. They were amazed to find more arrowheads, vases and large stones which look like tools that the Indians may have used.

"I'm going to start copying these drawings," Beth said, as she knelt next to the big vase.

"I will make a drawing of the entire washout and show where everything is located," Mark replied.

"That's a great idea," said Beth. "Timmy, you and Annie help him."

Beth copied the drawings that were engraved on the large vase and turned to a new page in her notebook to start the next vase. Sam helped her pull the sandy dirt from around the second vase to expose the drawings. Beth poured water from her water bottle to wash away the remaining sand.

"I hear a boat coming," Timmy said, "it must be Mom and Dad."

"I can't wait for them to see what we have found!" Annie said excitedly.

Everyone continued with their task, awaiting the arrival of their mother and father.

Mark took a tape measure from his backpack, and with the help of Timmy and Annie, was mapping the location of their findings in the washout.

Beth was finishing the last of her drawings when she felt Sam tug on her shirt.

"What's up, buddy?" she said without looking up.

She felt another tug on her shirt.

"I said 'What's up?'"

Suddenly, she realized that it had become very quiet. The chatter of the others' voices as they worked on the map turned to silence.

As she looked over her shoulder to where the others were, she saw they were all standing still, staring at the opening of the washout behind her.

She continued to turn toward the opening. Her eyes squinted for just a moment as she began to adjust to the light.

The large figure startled her for just a moment. With her eyes now focused and adjusted to the bright light shining through the opening, she could see the figure of a large man. The darkness made it hard to see his face in the shadows, but she could make out two long, braided ponytails that hung in front of his shoulders with a brightly colored band that wrapped around his forehead.

She blinked her eyes again and shook her head. Staring at the opening, she was convinced that the man standing there was an American Indian.

CHAPTER FIVE

"Do not be alarmed," the man said in a deep voice.

The children stood frozen.

The stranger took a step forward out of the shadows into the opening, giving the children a better view of himself.

The long braids of hair that hung down in front of his shoulders were a silvery gray. The skin on his face looked aged. His eyes, a deep, dark brown, glistened above his high cheekbones. He wore an old denim shirt and blue jeans with a belt that appeared to be handwoven from beads and leather.

"I did not mean to frighten you," he said. "I am a friend of Mr. Jacobs. He told me I may find you here."

Upon saying that, he reached into the collar of his shirt and pulled out a small leather pouch with a clear window in front. It contained his picture and a small gold badge with writing under it.

"My name is Joe Hawkins, and I am with the Bureau of Indian Affairs."

He smiled at the children and waited for a response.

Sam stepped forward and looked up at the big man.

"Are you a real American Indian?" he asked.

"Yes, I am," the stranger replied. "And who might you be?"

"Samuel Carson, but everyone calls me Sam."

"It's a pleasure to meet you," the man said, reaching out his hand to Sam. "My friends call me Big Joe. And who might the rest of these adventurers be?" he asked.

Beth, Mark and Annie stepped forward next and introduced themselves.

Timmy came forward last.

"Are you really an American Indian?"

"Yes, I am."

"I've never met a real American Indian before," Timmy told him.

"I hear that a lot," he said laughing, as he extended his hand to Timmy.

"My name is Timmy."

"It is a pleasure to meet all of you."

Mr. Hawkins stood up straight and examined the washout.

"My friend Jacobs was right. You children have made quite the find here."

Beth stepped closer to the big man.

"I've never heard of the Bureau of Indian Affairs. What does it do?"

"The Bureau was established many years ago. It is one of the oldest government agencies ever established," he explained. "Our job is to work with all other government agencies with any matters that involve the Native American community."

"So, you will be able to tell us who this belonged to and why it is here?" Mark asked.

"That's why I came," he responded. "Another part of my job is to gather information about the tribes that have lived in this region of the country and try to find out more about their history."

Mr. Hawkins walked over and knelt beside the large piece of pottery.

"This is in excellent condition. It is very rare to find this large of a piece still intact."

Beth knelt beside him and pointed to the second vase they had found.

"This one wasn't exposed yesterday. We were concerned that the tide may do more damage to the site."

"I am afraid you are right," Mr. Hawkins replied.

Just then they heard the leaves rustling and a stick break near the opening. Seconds later, their mother and father appeared.

Their father held a branch up as their mother passed under it, bringing her in full view of the washout.

"Wow!" their mother exclaimed. "Look at this place."

Their father looked toward the children and saw the stranger kneeling next to the artifacts.

"You must be Big Joe," he said.

Mr. Hawkins stood and properly introduced himself, as the children's parents did the same.

"We've heard some wonderful things about you from Mr. Jacobs," the children's mother said.

"Now, what would that ornery old trapper have to say good about me?" Mr. Hawkins said smiling.

"No one better be talking about me in there," Mr. Jacobs said, entering through the opening into the washout.

Mr. Hawkins turned to see him with a huge smile on his face. Everyone could tell he was pleasantly surprised.

"How long has it been, my old friend?" the big man asked.

"Too long," the old trapper replied.

They greeted each other with a handshake and a big hug.

While the two old friends exchange small talk, Beth leaned over and whispered to Mark.

"Did you notice how noisy Mom, Dad and Mr. Jacobs were coming into the washout? There were twigs breaking and leaves rustling. But when Mr. Hawkins came in, we heard nothing."

"I know," Mark answered, "I'd like to know how he did that."

"Me, too," Beth replied.

Everyone began looking around the washout surprised at the number of artifacts that were exposed.

"What can we do to help?" the children's father asked Mr. Hawkins.

"Well," he replied, "if this is a sacred burial ground, we should try not to disturb it. I would like to take some pictures to bring to the State University. They may be able to gather enough data from these drawings to link them with a certain tribe."

"Can we do anything to help?" Mark asked.

"Absolutely," Mr. Hawkins replied. "I would like you and Beth to dig some more mud from around this large vase so I can get some good photos. And if I could, I would like to get you three to carefully dig out a few of these tools."

The three younger children agreed with excitement.

"And while you are digging," their new friend said, "Mr. Jacobs and I will look around to make sure we don't miss anything important."

Everyone began with their projects.

Beth and Mark patiently pulled dirt away from the large piece of pottery. They were amazed at how big it was. It appeared to be about fourteen to fifteen inches tall with the base widening out to almost ten inches in diameter.

"If this was used to haul water, it would have been a little heavy, wouldn't you think so, Mr. Hawkins," Beth asked as he made his way around the washout toward her.

"I doubt if a vase this size would have been used for water," Mr. Hawkins said. "Judging from the detailed drawings and the fine craftsmanship, I would have to say this was probably some type of ceremonial vase, maybe even a burial vase."

"What would a burial vase be used for?" Mark asked.

"Some of the tribes of long ago would cremate or burn the bodies of their chiefs and leaders after they died. They would gather their ashes and put them in a vase, such as that one, and bury it in their sacred area." Big Joe explained.

"Are you telling me there may be a dead person in this vase?" Beth questioned.

"If that is what the vase was used for," Mr. Hawkins answered, "there may be ashes of someone's remains in there."

"This just became really weird," Beth said to Mark.

Before Mark could reply, they heard Timmy yell with excitement.

"Big Joe, come see this!"

He walked over to where the younger children were digging with the help of their parents. He looked down to see a few large stone ax heads and a couple of long slender stones, probably spearheads.

"Those artifacts are in great shape," Mr. Hawkins said.

"Not those," Timmy exclaimed, "look at this."

He pointed to an object flush with the ground that appeared to be metal.

Mr. Hawkins ran his finger all the way around the object.

"Is this what I think it is?" he asked, as he took a knife from his belt and pried the object out of the ground.

"It's a metal ax blade," the children's father said, looking over Mr. Hawkins' shoulder.

"Yes, it is," replied Mr. Hawkins. "It is forged metal. This was made by a blacksmith."

"What would that be doing with all of these artifacts?" their mother asked.

"These Indian tribes must have had dealings with the settlers of this area," Mr. Hawkins answered.

"They sure did," Mr. Jacobs chimed in, "my grandfather used to tell me stories of the tribes that lived in these parts who would trade fresh fish and wild game with the merchant ships that sailed the river."

Mr. Hawkins stood and began nodding his head.

"If this is true," he began, "then I can guarantee you one thing, someone wrote about it. Somewhere in the courthouse archives or the library archives are answers to some of our questions."

"Do you know what tribe of American Indians they may have been?" Beth asked.

"I can't tell you for sure. The banks of this river were home to two different tribes that occupied the coastal region."

Mr. Hawkins began to tell them the history of the two tribes. The first was the Chitimacha tribe. The name Chitimacha meant 'people of many waters.' They lived mainly along the western river basin, throughout the many rivers and bayous. They were skilled fishermen and thrived along the waterways.

The other tribe was the Houmas Indians. They occupied much of the territory east of the river. They were a much smaller tribe that originated in the central part of the state. Territorial issues with other tribes forced them to move to the coastal region. They were very friendly and lived well among the original settlers of the region. They too were skilled fishermen.

Mr. Hawkins told the children as much as he could about the history of the two tribes.

When he finished talking, the children's mother stepped toward Mr. Hawkins.

"You know, Big Joe," she said smiling, "it's been quite a while since my class took a field trip. I would think spending the day in town digging through the archives department and the library might be a good class project for them."

"We do need to go in for a few supplies anyway," their father added. "And I also heard there was a new pizza place that opened in town. Maybe we could check it out for lunch."

"Yes!" The children screamed together.

"Well," Mr. Hawkins said, "that sounds like a plan. I'll head to the university first thing in the morning, and you guys can hit the archives and library."

"That sounds like a great plan," the children's father added.

CHAPTER SIX

The children awoke early the next morning, eager to take the trip into town. As soon as they finished their breakfast, they were underway.

The cool, early morning air made the boat ride to town quite chilly. The children bundled in their warm coats for the trip.

Beth took her usual position alongside her father. She loved to look at all the wildlife scurrying along the banks as the boat made its way through the bayous.

Mark nestled into his usual spot behind his mother, blocked from the wind, reading a book the entire boat trip to town.

And of course, the two youngest children were being entertained by the antics of their brother Timmy. The children were not allowed to stand or walk around the boat while they were traveling, so Timmy would usually find something fairly calm to do. Today he had taken a round cap off of a plastic milk jug, put it over his eye and amused his brother and sister by acting like a pirate.

As they made their way around the last curve of the bayou and entered the big river, Beth could see all of the familiar sights of town.

Shrimp boats tied along the docks were unloading their fresh catch. Delivery trucks filled with supplies, nets and ice made their way up and down the pier.

A tugboat, struggling against the swift current, pushed a fuel barge up river. Seagulls flew close behind the tug, hoping to grab a fish being washed up in the murky water.

Their father brought the boat to an idle as they neared the landing. He waved to a couple of fishermen making their way out.

After they docked and secured the boat, they made their way to the parking lot where their truck was parked.

"We will have to make a trip to the hardware store and the grocery store before we go back," their father said.

"That's fine," their mother answered. "The library doesn't open until nine o'clock. That gives us thirty minutes," she said looking at her watch. "Let's go to the hardware store first, the library next and then the grocery store after lunch."

"And pizza for lunch," Annie said, licking her lips.

"Yes," her father said smiling, "pizza for lunch."

As much as the children enjoyed going to the hardware store, today they were anxious to gather their supplies and get to the library. After they checked everything off of their list, the children hurried to the front of the store with their parents.

"And what brings you all to town on this fine day."

The children immediately recognized the voice of Mr. Haynes, the store's owner.

"Just picking up a few supplies," the children's father answered, stepping forward to greet Mr. Haynes.

"Well, it is sure nice seeing you folks again," the store owner said. "But you all came in too early today. My lovely wife doesn't come in to help until midmorning, and you know how much she enjoys seeing these children."

"We're sorry we missed her," the children's mother replied. "Please make sure to give her our best."

"I will surely do that," Mr. Haynes responded, "and you make sure to come see me again soon."

"We will," their father said.

The children all said goodbye to the store owner and began to make their way to the next destination.

When they reached the library, the excitement they felt the day before returned.

The archives department was set off to the rear right corner of the library. The children quickly made their way to the corner and set up their workstation at the table nearest the archives.

Beth and Mark unloaded their backpacks. They placed the drawings of the vases along with the map of the washout on the table.

"And what can we do to help?" the children's father asked, standing next to their mother.

"What do you mean?" Mark replied with a puzzled looked.

"Well," their mother said, "your father and I have talked about it, and we feel this is your project. We would like to help you with your plans."

"Awesome," Beth said. "Give us just a minute to put together a plan and then we'll get started."

Moments later they were ready to go.

"Okay," Beth said to her parents, "the girls are going to work in the library trying to find information on local tribes and also trying to match the drawings."

"And the boys," Mark quickly followed, "are going to search the city archives for any articles or writings about the American Indian tribes that once lived in our area."

Annie raised her hand to speak next.

"Mom is one of the girls, and Dad is one of the boys," she said proudly.

"Thank you for clearing that up for us," her father said smiling.

The others laughed as they split into their teams and went to work.

The first thirty minutes showed little progress, but the children remained diligent and did not get discouraged.

Mark's team was the first to find something of importance. An internet search found a newspaper article over one hundred years old that someone had written about merchants traveling along the river and trading with local American Indian tribes. The article did not give many details, but it gave them hope that more existed.

Soon after, the girls located a book filled with details about the American Indian tribes of Southern Louisiana. The book contained a great deal of useful information. They placed the book in the center of the table. Any book in that stack would be checked out to return home with them.

The boys continued making progress. Their father made copies of each of the articles that they found so that they would have the information to take with them.

Everyone was so involved with their work that no one noticed it was well after twelve o'clock.

The children's mother was the first to realize the time.

"Hey guys," she said, "I thought we were going to have pizza for lunch."

"Is it time?" Timmy said, rubbing his stomach with a smile.

"I think we're just about finished here," their father responded.

"And I think we've found about all we are going to find," their mother added.

"Maybe you all can show us what you found while we eat lunch," Beth said.

"Yeah, that would be great," Mark answered, "we've got some really cool stuff."

"Beth, why don't you and Mark go check out the books we've picked out while the rest of us pick up and put things back like we found them," the children's mother said.

Everyone eagerly began their tasks. Ten minutes later they were out of the library and on their way to get pizza.

"So, Dad, what's the name of the new pizza place?" Beth asked.

"I don't know," he replied. "Deputy Cook told me about it. He said it was owned by a local family."

The restaurant location was only two blocks away, so they decided to walk. Briefly stopping at the truck, Beth put the books they checked out inside. Mark kept the copies he made to share with everyone while eating their lunch.

The chill in the air they felt that morning had been warmed by the sun in a cloudless sky, making it a perfect day to take a walk. While walking, the children exchange comments about the things they discovered at the library.

It was just before one o'clock when they rounded the corner coming in full view of the restaurant.

The building looked like a typical pizza parlor. The original name of the establishment that had been there before was covered with a small canvas. A new sign hung just below it, bordered with flashing decorative lights. And across the sign, painted in bright red, were the words 'Bubba's Pizza Palace.'

"Well, here we are," their father said.

"Are you sure this is the place?" their mother asked.

"It has to be," he said smiling. "It's the only pizza place in town."

"Isn't 'Bubba' an Italian name?" Mark said laughing.

"Sounds Italian to me," Timmy said rubbing his belly.

Their father held the door as they walked into the restaurant. The smell of freshly baked pizza filled the room.

The inside of the building bustled with activity. Tables covered with red and white checkered tablecloths filled the center of the room. The left and back walls were lined with booths. Off to the right were the kitchen, a serving area and the checkout counter. A small group of people, waiting to pay their bills, stood in line.

Just then they notice a young lady behind the register waving at them. Beth and Mark recognized her immediately. It was Sarah Haynes, the hardware store owner's daughter.

"I'll be with you guys in just one moment," she said over the noise of the busy restaurant.

"Take your time," the children's father said, "we're in no hurry."

The children's parents had known Sarah since she was a young girl. She grew up working in her father's hardware store. In the afternoons she could usually be found sitting behind the front counter at the store doing her homework and waiting on customers. Mr. Haynes, her father, recently told them on one of their visits to the store that she was now attending the local college near them.

"Sorry to keep you waiting," Sarah said, as she approached them a few minutes later.

"No problem," the children's mother replied. "It's good to see you. How have you been?"

"A little busy, but good," Sarah said with a smile.

"And how is college?" the children's father asked.

"I love it," Sarah replied. "I have a two-hour break in the middle of the day so I work here for lunch. Not only is the pay pretty good," she said as she lowered her voice and leaned in toward the children, "but you also get all the pizza you can eat for free."

She smiled and winked at the children.

They all smiled and giggled, well, all except for Timmy. There was no way a ten-year-old boy with a love for life and an equally strong love for pizza was going to let a comment like that go without a response.

He leaned in toward Sarah raising one eyebrow.

"Now that's what I'm talking about," he said.

Sarah tried momentarily not to laugh out loud, but she could not contain it. She burst into laughter, causing everyone else to do the same.

"All right," Sarah said, still laughing, "let me get you all to a table."

She walked them across the restaurant and seated them at a large table in the center of the main dining area.

"Someone will be with you shortly to take your order," Sarah said, as she hurried back to the front counter.

Everyone was hungry, which helped them agree quickly on what they were going to eat. After placing their order, they began discussing the items they found at the library and archives department.

Mark brought his backpack, which contained all of the copies they made at the archives. His father asked him to take out one article that they found about a burial ground. The article was from a local paper written in

April of 1909. The author wrote the article after interviewing an elderly American Indian who grew up living along the banks of the mighty river which flowed along their land.

The children's father began reading the article to the children and then paused for a moment.

"This is the part you need to pay close attention to," he said, raising his finger in the air, "'The tribes of this region often spoke of a sacred burial ground. It was located near the high ground where a mighty river took two paths, one heading to the great waters and the other into the sunset.'"

He stopped reading and grabbed a paper napkin from the table. He unfolded it and began drawing on it with a pen he removed from his pocket.

"All right, my little adventurers," he said, looking at the children, "let's put this into a drawing. We know the river runs almost due south once it leaves town. And what would be the great waters they talked about in the article?"

"It would have to be the Gulf of Mexico," Mark responded.

"That's right," his father said, as he continued drawing on the napkin. "And one of the waterways headed into the sunset."

"That would mean due west," Beth said excitedly.

"Right again," her father said. He continued drawing on the napkin. "And if the description of the sacred burial ground is accurate, then this is what we are looking for."

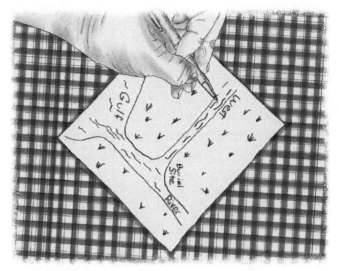

He held the napkin up facing the children.

"That's a map of Willow Hammock," Beth and Mark screamed at the same time.

"So, if this is the burial ground they spoke of," the children's mother said, "then everything Mr. Hawkins needs should be in this article."

"That is correct," their father answered. "So, our next step is to contact Mr. Hawkins. We will tell him of our findings and then find out what he wants us to do to preserve the site from further tidal damage."

"That needs to be done as soon as possible," Beth replied, "before more artifacts get washed away."

"I will try to reach Mr. Hawkins and arrange a meeting with him tomorrow," their father said.

He looked up and saw a waiter approaching the table carrying two large pizzas.

"But I think right now," he said smiling, "it's time to eat."

The waiter set the two pizzas in the center of the table, looking curiously at the papers and map lying on the table.

"This looks like some pretty interesting stuff," he said.

"We're adventurers," Timmy said proudly.

"Is that so?" the waiter said.

He glanced at the paperwork again and then backed away from the table.

"Enjoy your pizza," he said to them.

The family enjoyed the wonderful meal. They talked about their plans for the rest of the day and their next chance to meet with Mr. Hawkins.

When they finished their meal, they said goodbye to Sarah and went to gather the rest of their supplies.

Two hours later, they were loading their boat, ready to get underway.

With beautiful weather and calm winds, they decided to take the river back to Willow Hammock instead of the inside route through the smaller bayous.

The information they discovered at the library made for exciting conversations on the boat ride back to the houseboat. They wondered what it would have been like traveling the same waterway they were traveling a hundred years earlier, or maybe even two hundred years earlier. Small Indian villages scattered along the riverbanks, merchant sailings ships traveling through the muddy waters, and maybe even a pirate ship lurking in the distance under the cover of darkness.

Their imaginations ran wild the entire way home.

And after a long day, bedtime came early. The children drifted off to sleep, thinking about the adventure that could be waiting for them.

****

Early the next morning their father was able to reach Mr. Hawkins by cell phone. They made arrangements for all of them to meet at the washout at two o'clock that afternoon.

By one o'clock, Beth and Mark had completed all of the schoolwork they missed the day before and finished their scheduled lessons.

"Can Mark and I go ahead of you all and look around," Beth pleaded with her mother.

"Go ahead," she said, "your father and I will take the boat with the others in a little while and meet you there."

Ten minutes later, Beth and Mark made their way along the riverbank, hurrying to reach the washout.

They were eager to tell Mr. Hawkins about the information they discovered at the library and the city archives.

"Do you think Mr. Hawkins was able to find out anything important from the university?" Mark asked.

"It will probably take them some time to research any information they have," Beth replied.

As they approached the entrance to the washout, Mark noticed fresh footprints.

"Mr. Hawkins must already be here," Mark said.

"I don't see his boat," Beth replied.

"Someone has been here," Mark told her. "Look at all of the footprints."

Mark lifted one of the low-lying branches to let his sister walk into the opening ahead of him.

He heard Beth gasp as she stepped into the musty washout. He quickly stepped to her side to see what was wrong. Mark stood there motionless with his mouth wide open, unable to speak.

"Why would someone do this?" Beth said, with her voice shaking.

The site that they discovered, the site that the Native American Indians who once lived there considered sacred, was ruined. Holes were dug throughout the washout. Mud had been thrown everywhere, and not a single artifact remained.

CHAPTER SEVEN

"We have to find out who did this," Mark said, as they sat on the shell reef, waiting for the others to arrive.

"I'm sure Mr. Hawkins will know who to call to get help," Beth replied.

"We can't let whoever did this get away with it," Mark said angrily.

They heard a boat approaching in the distance.

"Here comes Mom and Dad with the others", she said, hopping to her feet.

"And there's a boat right behind them," Mark added. "That must be Mr. Hawkins."

As the two boats neared, Beth and Mark could see Mr. Jacobs on the bow of Mr. Hawkins' boat. The two children walked to the water's edge to meet their parents and the others.

From the look on Beth and Mark's face, the children's father knew immediately that something was not right.

"What's wrong?" he asked with concern.

"Everything's gone," Beth said, with her voice beginning to shake again.

"What do you mean everything is gone?" their mother said, as she hopped from the boat to console Beth.

"Someone robbed the site," Mark said. "They took everything. There's nothing left."

Mr. Hawkins heard the entire conversation. As soon as his boat touched the riverbank, he leaped out and ran into the washout. He came out moments later with a look of despair on his face.

"Everyone stay in your boat," he said, "we don't want to disturb any evidence that could have been left behind by whoever did this."

Mr. Hawkins walked over to his boat and sat on the bow. He remained there silent.

"What do we need to do?" Mr. Jacobs said, taking a seat next to his friend.

"Nothing right now," he said, "we just need to contact the local authorities and let them know about the theft."

"I can take care of that," the children's father responded. "I will take my family back to the houseboat and call the Sheriff's Department."

"That would be a good thing," Mr. Hawkins said.

Mark quickly ran to the edge of the bank where his father's boat was parked.

"But Dad," Mark pleaded, "we just can't leave. We have to find out who did this."

Mr. Hawkins slowly stood and walked over to where Mark was standing. He put his hand on Mark's shoulder and spoke to him softly.

"The only thing we can do right now is to let the local authorities do their job. That will be the best chance we have to catch those who are involved in this."

Mr. Hawkins walked back to his boat and took a seat.

The two older children stood there watching the big man. He seemed very distant, staring out over the open water.

Everyone loaded into the boat as their father started the engine and began backing away from the reef.

Mr. Hawkins did not move an inch. The children could see that he was more than just upset. He was hurting deep down inside.

****

Just before dark, Mr. Jacobs stopped at the houseboat to update the family about the events of the afternoon.

He told them that the sheriff's department sent two detectives to start the investigation. They had taken plaster casts of the footprints found near the entrance of the washout. Some evidence was also collected, which included an empty water bottle that they hoped would contain some fingerprints.

"They said they would come by here sometime tomorrow afternoon to meet with all of you," Mr. Jacobs said. "They would like to see if there is anything that you could add to help them with the investigation."

"That will be fine," the children's father said, "anything we can do to help."

Mr. Jacobs could see the disappointment on the children's faces. He walked over to where they were seated.

"You know," he said, "I have a real good feeling everything is going to work out just fine. Those two detectives looked very eager and Mr. Hawkins is a very determined man."

The children smiled at Mr. Jacobs but remained silent.

"They're going to be just fine," the children's mother said, walking over and putting her hands on Beth and Mark's shoulders.

"If there is one thing that I know about living at Willow Hammock, tomorrow will not only bring a whole new day, but it will also bring a new adventure with it," their old friend told them.

****

The next morning the children were back on their regular schedule. Their mother made an extra effort to keep them focused on their schoolwork. The children's father adjusted his work schedule to be at the houseboat when the detectives arrived. It also worked out well to have him there to keep the younger children occupied when they finished their schoolwork.

Shortly after lunch, Beth noticed a boat nearing the camp as she cleared her desk.

She recognized Deputy Cook and his patrol boat immediately.

"Mom, Deputy Cook is here. Can I go tell Dad?" she yelled.

"Yes," she replied, "it might be a good time to take a break anyway."

Beth quickly made her way to her father's workshop to let him know of the deputy's arrival and then made her way to the dock.

She noticed that there were two other men in the boat with him. Both of them wore khaki pants and pullover shirts with a Sheriff's Department star embroidered on the front. She hoped that they were the detectives sent to ask about the stolen artifacts, and she also hoped that they were bringing some good news with them.

Her father, along with Annie and Sam, met her at the dock as the boat approached. Beth could see Deputy Cook's face light up when he noticed the two children waving to him.

The children had known Tom Cook, or Deputy Cook as they called him, for their entire lives. He had been patrolling the waters of their area for close to thirty years. At sixty years of age, he was tall and thin, with a dark complexion and short silvery gray hair.

His patrol brought him by Willow Hammock around midmorning every two weeks. The children's mother would usually let them take a break from their schoolwork for a short time so they could visit with the deputy. They would sit and listen to all of the exciting events that occurred during the deputy's patrol. The children's mother and father enjoyed the visits also. The stories would usually end with the deputy teaching the children a lesson or two about how to avoid the bad situations he dealt with while on patrol.

Today, however, there would be no visit with the deputy. As soon as the detectives stepped onto the dock, they quickly introduced themselves to the children's father and asked if they could sit down with the family to ask questions. Moments later, they were sitting around the kitchen table.

The children's mother told the three youngest they could play outside, and that she would call them if they were needed.

The two detectives pulled out their pads of paper and ink pens and began by asking everyone their name and age. Next, they asked if someone could explain to them how they found the artifact site.

Their father told them about the children finding the site while exploring at the point. He tried to give them as much information as he could about the events leading up to the day when the site had been robbed.

The two detectives made notes while the children's father talked. When their father finished talking, the detectives asked if they knew of anyone else who had knowledge of the site or if they noticed anyone near the site.

They made a few more notes and then thanked the family for their time.

As the two gentlemen stood to excuse themselves, Mark bolted from his seat.

"Is that all?" he responded.

"That's all for now," one of the detectives said.

"But you didn't tell us about any clues you have and who you think could have been involved," Mark told them.

The detective put his hand on Mark's shoulder.

"We're just getting started," he said, smiling at him. "As a matter of fact, there is a field detective at the artifact site as we speak making more plaster casts of the footprints and gathering information."

"Really?" Mark said.

"Yes, really," the detective replied.

"When can we go back to the point?" Beth asked.

"Well," the detective said thinking, "you will have to give us a couple days to make sure we don't miss any evidence. And even after that, if you do decide to go back to the site, I would advise that you go with your parents, just for your own safety."

"I think we agree with that completely," the children's father said.

"Great," the detective replied, extending his hand out to the children's father.

"Please let us know if you find out anything important," their father said, shaking the detective's hand.

"You will be the first to know," the detective replied politely.

Everyone walked to the wharf with Deputy Cook and the two detectives to say goodbye.

As the officer's boat pulled away from the dock, Timmy was the first to speak.

"So, do they know who done it?"

Beth grabbed his hand and looked him straight in the face.

"Do they know who did it," she said, putting an emphasis on the word 'did'.

Timmy looked at her with confusion.

"How would I know?" he said shrugging his shoulders. "Y'all were the ones talking with them."

"Uuugh!!" Beth moaned loudly, as she marched off into the yard.

"So, what's up with her?" Timmy said, clueless to what had just happened.

"Why don't you all go out in the yard and play," the children's mother said, trying not to laugh. "I'll go fix you all a snack."

The children made their way to the swing set. The three older children sat on the swings in the middle while Annie and Sam took the ones on each end.

Annie and Sam were too young to fully understand the situation they were involved in. The two were both carefree. Annie, lying back on her swing with her arms fully extended, watched the white puffy clouds drift by. Sam took his favorite position, with the seat of the swing tucked into his belly and his knees pulled up under him. Swinging softly, he fixed his eyes upon the ground, searching for any kind of bug that just might wander his way.

The three older children sat on their swings talking with each other.

"How would anyone even know about the washout?" Beth asked.

"I don't know," Mark answered.

"Maybe someone at the library overheard us," Beth replied.

"There was no one there except us for most of the morning," Timmy said.

"Well," Mark replied, "even if someone heard us talking, they still would not have known where to go."

"Yeah," Beth agreed, "even if they heard us, they still would need a map to know where the site was."

"But we didn't find any maps, did we?" Timmy questioned.

Suddenly, Mark sprang up from his seat.

"There was a map!" he yelled. "The one that Dad drew on the napkin at the pizza place."

"That's right," Timmy said, "and do you remember that waiter asking the questions?"

"Yes," Mark responded, "that could be the guy who stole the artifacts from the washout."

"Wait, wait, wait," Beth said, trying to calm the boys. "Mom and Dad would not be too happy if they heard us accusing someone without proof. I think it is okay to consider that a possibility, but we don't point the finger at anyone until we have some kind of proof."

The two boys sat back on their swings, thinking about what their sister had said.

"How do we get proof?" Mark asked.

"I don't know," Beth replied. "They've already stolen everything there. If the detectives do not find anything, I doubt if we will either."

"Maybe we can set a trap!" Timmy said with excitement.

"Were you listening to what I said," Beth responded. "They have no reason to come back. How would you get them to come to your trap?"

Annie had been sitting quietly the entire time the three older children were talking. Still leaning back, looking to the sky, she suddenly spoke.

"You've got to have bait."

"What?" Beth asked.

Annie pulled herself up straight and drug her feet along the ground, bringing her swing to a stop.

"You can't have a trap without bait, silly," she said.

Beth and Mark turned to each other and smiled.

"Annie, you're a genius," Beth said.

"I am?" Annie remarked.

"Yes, you are," Mark added.

CHAPTER EIGHT

The children, having spent most of the evening planning, eagerly started their schoolwork early the following morning. They knew there were still a few things their mother and father were going to have to agree with to make their plan work.

While serving breakfast, their mother noticed that the children were acting strangely.

"Does someone want to tell me what's going on?" she asked.

Mark kicked Beth under the table and nodded his head, trying to get her to talk.

"Well," Beth said, "we were kind of wondering…"

"Wondering about what, dear," her mother responded, smiling at their father.

"Well," she started again, "if we were to complete two lessons of schoolwork today, do you think it might be possible we could go to the library and go eat pizza again tomorrow?"

Their mother looked over at her husband.

"What do you think?" she asked.

"I don't see why not," he said, "but instead of pizza how about Chinese."

Their father loved to eat Chinese food but rarely had the opportunity.

"We really would like to go back to the pizza place," Mark said.

"But I thought you all loved Chinese food," their father responded.

"No, you're the one who loves Chinese food, remember," his wife said smiling.

"I think I lost this debate before it really got started," he said laughing, as he got up from the table.

"Oh, Dad, one more thing," Mark quickly added.

"What's that?" their father responded.

"You know those night vision cameras you use for tracking wildlife movement?" Mark asked. "Do you think we can borrow one?"

"I don't see why not," he answered. "I have one in the workshop that needs fresh batteries."

"Yes!" Timmy said excitedly.

Their father looked over to their mother and then back at the children.

"Is there anything your mother and I need to know about?" he asked curiously.

"Not yet," Beth replied. "But we promise we will tell you as soon as there is."

The children spent the better part of the day finishing two days of schoolwork. Even Annie and Sam continued working throughout the day. Later in the afternoon, some light rain showers passed over. Rain usually meant extra schoolwork, since they were unable to play outside. So, staying in to do some extra work would have kept them occupied anyway.

After supper that night, the children returned to their room to work on their plan.

"All right," Mark said, "does everyone know what to do?"

"We better make sure we do," Beth answered. "We only have one chance to make this work."

"I know what Sam and I are supposed to do," Timmy said. "We have to find a book about pirates to check out at the library."

"That's right," Mark replied. "I will make sure we have a copy of the article we found about the merchants trading with the Indians. And when I'm done with that, I'll find a book about metal detectors."

"Perfect," Beth said. "Annie and I will find a book about gold coins to check out. And when we get to the pizza place, we need to make sure that everything is left in plain sight on the table."

"What happens if the guy we are setting the trap for is not working?" Timmy asked.

"We just have to hope that everything works out the way we've planned," Beth answered.

Just then the children's mother appeared in the doorway.

"Okay, guys," she said, "brush your teeth and say your prayers. It is bedtime."

Their father stuck his head over her shoulder, peering at the children as they sat on the floor.

"Are you sure there's nothing we need to know?" he asked, looking curiously at them.

"Not yet," Beth answered, "but we promise we will let you know as soon as there is."

****

The next morning the children arose early, ready to get their day started. Their mother was pleased that she did not have to remind anyone to make their beds or to clean their room. Beth and Mark even volunteered to do the breakfast dishes to make sure they left on time.

The boat ride into town that morning was a bit chilly. Beth realized that the rain the day before must have been part of a cold front. Occasionally, the rising sun would appear through breaks in the trees, briefly warming her face before it would disappear again behind the willow trees that lined the banks of the bayous.

As they neared the landing, the children's father slowed the boat. Timmy quickly stood alongside Beth to see the early morning activity on the docks. He saw the flash of a welding machine on a large shrimp boat that was being repaired. Another smaller boat parked next to it was being loaded with supplies from a grocery truck.

When they reached the other end of the docks where the smaller boats were moored, Beth noticed a group of crab fishermen crowded onto the docks. As the boat drifted a little closer, she immediately recognized the two men talking to them.

"Look, Dad," Beth yelled, "it's the two detectives who came to the houseboat with Deputy Cook."

"It sure is," he replied, "I wonder what they're doing here."

The children's father positioned their boat alongside the dock in an opening between two fishing boats. Mark and Timmy jumped onto the dock and secured the boat to the pier. Beth helped her younger brother and sister onto the pier and then climbed up herself. They all removed their life jackets and handed them to their father.

Mark saw one of the detectives excuse himself from the group as he began walking toward them.

"Hello, everyone," he said smiling as he approached the group.

"Hello," the children replied back.

"Seeing you here just saved me a boat ride this afternoon," the detective said.

"Do you have some news for us?" Timmy asked curiously.

"Yes, I do," he answered, "but I'm afraid it's not good news."

"I hope it's not too bad," the children's father said, as he stepped forward between the children and greeted the detective.

"It seems our thieves have struck again," the detective said with some disappointment. "Apparently, last night the cemetery on Oak Island was robbed. None of the graves were dug up, but they did take some headstones, statues and vases that were there."

The children listened without saying a word. They knew where the cemetery that the detective spoke of was located.

Oak Island, which was located across the river from town, had once been home to a large settlement. Most of the people who lived there were trappers and fishermen and their families. The children's mother had an uncle and aunt who lived on the island many years before. But the only way to the island was by boat, which eventually caused the settlement to be abandoned.

"Do you think it was the same people who robbed us?" the children's father asked.

"We're pretty sure it is," the detective answered. "A set of the footprints we found at the site near your place matched perfectly with one of the sets from the site at Oak Island."

"Was there any other evidence that was helpful?" the children's mother asked.

"Not really," he replied, "but we are looking into some information we just received last night."

"Is it anything you can share with us?" their father asked.

"I guess it wouldn't hurt anything to tell you," the detective answered. He stepped closer to them, lowering his voice a little. "It seems your friend Mr. Hawkins uncovered a similar circumstance as yours near a reservation about fifty miles north of here. When we contacted the local authorities, we found out there have been five thefts in that area that matched the description of these."

"Wow," Mark said, "these guys sound like professionals."

"They sure do," the detective said, "and after the incident at Oak Island, we're pretty sure they're still in this area."

"That's good," Mark replied, looking over at Beth.

"Why is that good?" the detective asked curiously.

Mark looked back at the detective not knowing what to say. As he stood there with his mouth open, he wondered if he had just blown their whole plan.

When Beth realized what her brother said, she quickly responded.

"I think what he's trying to say is that if they are still close by, you have a better chance of catching them. Isn't that right, Mark?" Beth said, poking him with her finger in his back.

"That's right," Mark said, nodding his head.

"Well, I guess you're right," the detective replied, still thinking about what the children had said. "One thing is for sure," he continued, "I can't catch them if I don't get back to work."

The detective said goodbye to them and returned to the group of fishermen on the dock.

The children and their parents walked across the parking lot to their vehicle.

As they walked, Beth brushed up against Mark and whispered in his ear.

"That was really smooth, Sherlock."

"Sorry," Mark replied sheepishly.

Their father did not have much of a supply list since they had just made a trip to town a few days before. But the things that were needed required them to make many different stops. Besides the grocery store and hardware store, their mother needed some things for the medicine cabinet from the drugstore, and their father needed a part for his airboat from the auto parts store.

Beth assured the other children that it would work out fine since they did not need much time at the library.

When they finally reached the library, everyone was eager to take care of their part in the plan. After convincing their parents that they should have a cup of coffee in the snack area, the children went to work. Beth showed Timmy how to use the library's computer to find a book by subject and sent him and Sam on their way. Then, she and Annie went to work on their own information.

By this time, Mark had already made a copy of the article they needed. He remembered the copy machine at the library required twenty-five cents to make a copy. He also remembered the machine was capable of enlarging the copy.

As he walked by Beth on his way to get his books, he showed her the copy he made.

"Do you think this was worth twenty-five cents?" Mark asked, holding up the copy of the article for Beth to see.

"Absolutely," she replied, taking the piece of paper from Mark to study it.

The article, which had once taken up two inches on a newspaper page, was now the size of a full sheet of paper. And at the top of the page, in big, bold print was the title of the article, 'LOCAL AMERICAN INDIAN TRIBES INVOLVED IN MERCHANT TRADING'.

In just a short amount of time, the children selected three books on each of their subjects and met at a large table in the middle of the library. Beth placed the books on the table in three rows.

"This is what we have to work with," she said. "It's all about the cover of the book. Which of these is most likely to catch someone's attention?"

As Beth pointed to each book, the others made comments about them. Within minutes they had picked the books they were going to use. They each went and put the books that were not chosen in the library's return cart.

When they returned to the table, Mark took the copy of the article out of his notebook and placed it in front of them.

They stared at the books next to the article. The first book, titled '*Pirates of the Gulf Coast,*' had a picture of a pirate ship on the cover. The second book told all about metal detectors. And the final book was all about antique coins, with a picture of an old gold coin on the cover.

"So, is this the bait?" Annie asked, looking at her three older siblings.

"This is the bait," Timmy replied.

"I think we are going to catch a big one," Annie said smiling.

"I hope you're right," Mark said, as he grabbed the books and headed to the librarian's desk.

"Now let's go get some pizza," Sam said.

****

As they turned into the parking lot of Bubba's Pizza Palace, Mark could see the concern on his older sister's face.

"I hope we didn't do all this for nothing," Beth said.

"He is going to be here," Mark replied, "I just know it."

When they walked through the front door, Sarah Haynes was the first to greet them.

"Back so soon," she said smiling, "you all must have really enjoyed the pizza last time."

"We sure did," their father replied. "Can you seat us at the same table?"

"Absolutely," she answered, "wait here, and I'll get some menus."

By this time the children had scanned the entire restaurant looking for the young man who waited on them the last time. Suddenly out of the kitchen door, he appeared, carrying a large tray with some salads and drinks on it.

Timmy, standing in front of the other children next to his mother and father, turned to them and gave a thumbs up.

Sarah seated them at the table and excused herself to get back to the counter.

Soon after, the waiter that they hoped for, approached the table with his notebook in hand.

Beth and Mark saw the expression on his face when he recognized the family.

"Well," he said with a slight stutter, "it's you guys again."

"Yes, we could not wait to get back," the children's father said laughing.

That seemed to set the waiter at ease.

"What can I get for you folks?" the waiter said.

The children's father placed their order just as he had done a few days before.

"I will be back with your drinks shortly," the waiter said, as he turned and headed for the kitchen.

Mark felt Beth nudge his foot under the table.

"Oh, Dad, we found some cool books at the library," he said. "I brought my book sack so we could show them to you."

"This looks pretty interesting," he said, taking the books from Mark as he passed them over the table.

He briefly looked at the cover of each book and then handed them back to Mark.

"I'll look at them more in detail when we get home," their father said. "But for now, you need to put them out so the waiter can see them when he returns with our drinks."

The children gasped and stared at their father and mother.

"How did you know that's what we were doing?" Beth asked.

"We are parents," their father said in a deep voice, raising his arms into the air. "We are all-knowing," he continued, lowering his arm slowly to his sides.

"All right," their mother said laughing. She leaned forward and whispered to the children. "Your father and I had our suspicions also. We put two and two together and kind of figured out what was going on with you all."

"But don't worry," their father added very seriously, holding his hands in the air. "The only reason we're here today is because your mother and I think your plan is a good one."

"And you also figured out what we're planning to do with your night vision camera?" Mark asked.

"Sure did," their father said grinning. "I even changed the mounting straps to fit the smaller willows at the point."

"But first things first," the children's mother said. "Let's act normal and get through this meal. Oh, and by the way, here comes our waiter."

The waiter returned to the table with their drinks. At first, he seemed a bit distracted. When he worked his way around the table to where Mark was sitting, his eyes locked onto the books. Beth saw her mother grin when the waiter almost spilled Mark's drink. The books and article definitely caught his attention. After their pizza had been served, he returned to the table at least a dozen times to refill drinks and check on his customers. Each time he returned he studied the article and books that were lying on the table.

Everything at the restaurant went as well as could be expected. By the time they finished their meal, the waiter's curiosity had them convinced that he was somehow involved.

****

The trip back to the houseboat was filled with excitement. They were sure that their plan was going to work. The children asked their father if they could all return to the washout that afternoon to mount the camera.

As soon as they unloaded their supplies, they jumped back into the boat and made their way to the shell reef at the river's edge.

"How many pictures will it take?" Timmy asked as the boat slid along the water.

"I put an empty memory card in it, so it should have room to take pictures all night long" he answered. "The way the camera takes pictures," he began to explain, "is from movement in front of the lens. And it will take a picture every thirty seconds as long as it senses movement."

"Is there any way they will notice it?" Beth asked.

"There is no flash," the father began to answer, "but it does make a small clicking sound like a small twig breaking."

"Do you think they will hear it?" Mark asked.

"I'm hoping the frogs and crickets will be out," he replied. "They should make enough racket to avoid hearing it."

After helping their father pull their boat ashore at the point, the children ran to the path between the two shell reefs that led to the washout. In the short time since they'd last been there, the path had widened and one of the trees that once lined the opening was now leaning over, with the roots exposed from being washed away by the tides.

As they entered the dark, damp site, the children noticed that the entire clearing had a small layer of water covering it.

Beth heard her parents walking in behind her.

"Dad, look what happened," she said.

"Goodness," he exclaimed, "I would never have thought the tides would have done this much damage so quickly."

"We are going to have to do something," their mother said.

"No matter what happens with your plan tonight," their father responded, "we must get permission from Mr. Hawkins and the local authorities to close up that opening to protect the site from the tides."

Their father stepped gently into the water.

"Listen up," he said. "Mark and I will mount the camera near the back while the rest of you look around to see if anything else has been exposed. But walk slowly and step softly," he added, "we don't want to stir up too much mud."

Mark and his father had just begun to tighten the straps of the camera on the tree they chose when they heard Annie call out.

"Mom, come see, over here!" she yelled excitedly.

Her mother eased her way through the shallow water. Annie was gently removing sand from around a small object in the murky water.

"It looks like she found a small clay vase or jar buried on its side in the mud," she told the others.

"Well," their father said with some hesitation, "I guess we better dig it up and take it with us. If the thieves do return tonight, there is no sense in leaving it for them."

"Beth, why don't you and Annie dig this out, and I will continue looking with Timmy and Sam," her mother told her.

As Beth and Annie began pulling the mud away from around the vase, Beth noticed that instead of drawings, two wavy lines were engraved around the center.

It took very little time to dig the jar from the soft mud. By the time Mark and his father finished mounting the camera, the rest of the family had found one stone ax head and five arrowheads to add to the vase Annie found.

"Well guys," the children's father said, "I think we've done all we can do here. Let's gather up the artifacts you found and head home."

The excitement in the houseboat lasted well into the night. Finally, at nine o'clock the children's father decided it was time to shut things down.

"It's time for bed," he yelled from the kitchen.

"Are everyone's teeth brushed?" they heard their mother yell from her bedroom.

"Yes, ma'am," they all yelled back.

Their father walked into their room and hugged them all good night. "Make sure you say your prayers and get some sleep. We may have a big day ahead of us tomorrow."

****

The children were overwhelmed with excitement on the boat ride to the point the following morning.

Their father passed up the place where the two shell reefs came together and circled the outside of the point. He explained to everyone that he wanted to be sure there was no one at or near the point. When he felt safe that there was no one in the area, they returned and parked the boat.

The children jumped from the boat and ran to the entrance of the washout.

"Mom, Dad, it's full of fresh footprints," Timmy yelled.

Their parents joined them at the opening as they all walked into the washout together. There were six fresh mounds of shoveled dirt.

"It looks like your plan worked," their father said.

"Dad, can me and Beth check the camera?" Mark asked.

"That will be fine," their father answered.

The two older children ran to the back of the washout, splashing water everywhere. They then disappeared into a small group of willow trees near the edge.

It was silent for a few moments.

Suddenly, they heard Mark's voice.

"Yes!" he yelled.

"We got them, Dad," they heard Beth yell, "the camera took eighty-four pictures."

CHAPTER NINE

The ride back to the houseboat was overwhelming for the children's parents. Each of the children were giving their own plan on how to catch the thieves.

Needless to say, Timmy's plan involved knocking down doors, throwing people to the ground and screaming "You're Busted!"

Both Beth and Mark's plans were made up of more traps and clever schemes.

Sam liked Timmy's idea but somehow wanted to add riding a horse.

And of course, quiet little Annie was the last to speak up. "I think I would call Deputy Cook and see if he has a plan," she said.

"I think I'm going to have to agree with Annie on this one," the children's father said.

"But Dad," Mark said, "what if they won't let us get involved?"

"That will be their decision," he answered. "And I assure you that they are not going to do anything that would put us in harm's way."

Their father slowed the boat as they neared the dock at the houseboat.

"Okay, kids," he said, "each of you go get your backpacks and make sure you have an extra set of clothes and your toothbrush. I'll lock up everything and then contact Deputy Cook to see if he can meet us at the landing."

"Yes, sir," the children said.

"So, do you think we will have to stay in town tonight?" Beth asked excitedly.

"Maybe so," her mother answered her, "it's best to be prepared in any case."

The children beamed with enthusiasm as they readied for the trip to town.

"Everything is secure outside," they heard their father saying as he walked into the houseboat. "How's everyone doing in here?"

"I'm packed and so are you," his wife said, handing him his overnight bag, as she walked out of the bedroom smiling.

"Thank you, dear," he said smiling back at her. "And what about the vase and the items we…"

"Already packed," his wife said before he could even finish his sentence.

"Dad," he heard Beth yell from the front porch, "have you called Deputy Cook yet?"

"Not yet," he answered.

"Don't bother," she said laughing. "He's tying his boat to the dock right now."

"Well, that's convenient," their father said, walking out the door to greet the deputy.

With the rest of the family right behind him, their father made his way along the dock. Everyone had a feeling that something must have happened for the deputy to show up unexpectedly.

"I was just getting ready to try to reach you," their father told Deputy Cook as he greeted him at the dock. "We have something that might be of interest to you and your detectives."

"And what would that be?" the deputy replied.

Their father reached into his pocket and pulled out the memory card from the game camera. He held the card between his finger and thumb and smiled at the deputy.

"It seems our thieves may have returned to the point last night," he told Deputy Cook.

The deputy looked at their father in amazement.

"And you have it on that card?" he replied.

"We have a really good feeling that's what is on here," their father said.

"Why would they have returned to the site again?" the deputy asked, looking a bit confused.

"Well," their father said looking down at the children, "it seems a group of junior detectives may have set a little bait and trap plan."

"You children never cease to amaze me," the deputy said, smiling at the children.

"And what brings you out to see us so early in the morning?" the children's mother asked.

"Well," he said, as he knelt in front of the children, "I was sent here to get you guys. We need your help."

The children turned and looked at their parents, waiting to hear their response.

"I'm sure they would be willing to help in any way they can," their mother said smiling.

"Yes!" The children yelled, giving each other high fives.

"How soon before you folks can be ready to travel?"

"We are ready right now," their mother said smiling.

"Don't bother getting your boat," the deputy said to their father, "this is official police business, and you folks are riding with me."

The children, giggling with excitement, ran to get their life jackets and backpacks. Within minutes, everyone was loaded into Deputy Cook's boat, as they eased away from the dock.

The children's parents sat on a small bench seat in the rear of the boat with Sam between them. Beth, Mark and Annie sat in the front of the boat, holding onto the rail that ran along the top of the hull. And, of course, Timmy was standing alongside Deputy Cook, who was driving from his center console.

The big boat climbed onto the surface of the water as Deputy Cook pushed the throttle forward.

Timmy tapped the deputy on the hand to get his attention.

"Didn't you say this was official police business?" Timmy asked, pointing to two switches on the driver's dashboard marked 'siren' and 'lights.'

"I sure did," Deputy Cook said, smiling at him, "go ahead and turn them on."

Timmy reached forward and gently pushed the two switches to the 'ON' position.

Instantly, the red and blue flashing lights mounted over the motor turned on, followed by the muffled sound of a police siren.

Beth, Mark and Annie turned around as soon as they heard the siren. They quickly notice Timmy standing next to the deputy grinning from ear to ear.

"It looks like there's not going to be much river traffic this morning," Deputy Cook said to Timmy as they rounded the point and entered the river. "I think we can turn the siren off, but leave the lights on."

"Yes, sir," Timmy said, reaching to turn the switch off.

The deputy turned to see how his passengers in the rear of the boat were doing.

"Thank you," the children's mother yelled over the roar of the motor.

"I don't really use the siren much," the deputy said, "it's a bit annoying."

"I agree," their mother said, smiling at the deputy.

The ride to town did not seem to take long at all.

As the boat neared the docks, the children noticed one of the detectives that had come to visit them waiting there. When he saw that the children recognized him, he waved to them.

"I was hoping you would agree to help us with our investigation," the detective said as Deputy Cook brought the boat alongside the dock.

"They've done more than that," Deputy Cook said. "It seems a certain group of junior detectives may have gotten some pictures of our thieves returning to the site on their land last night."

"How in the world did you do that?" the detective asked.

"It's a long story," the children's father said, "and I'm sure you have a lot of work to do, so we can tell you the details later."

"Where are the pictures?" the detective asked.

Beth unzipped a pocket in the front of her backpack and showed him the memory card.

"Our field technicians have a lab at headquarters that can print these pictures. Maybe you junior detectives can tell me how you did this while the lab develops the pictures."

"We sure will," Beth told him.

"Let's get to the station then," the detective said.

"Our vehicle is parked right over there," the children's father said, pointing across the parking lot.

"Great," the detective said, "Deputy Cook and I will escort you to the station."

"With lights and sirens," Timmy asked.

"Absolutely," the detective said laughing.

"We are ready when you are," their father said.

The detective did exactly what he said he would do and left his lights and siren on the entire way there. The children talked nonstop while their father followed the detective's car.

"What do you think they need our help for?" Beth asked.

"I have no idea," their father answered.

"Maybe they want us to set another trap," Mark said.

"Could be," their mother said turning around in her seat to see their reaction.

"Well, I hope they let us catch those thieves," Timmy said. "Because if they do," he added, "I'm ready."

He unzipped his backpack and pulled out his slingshot and a sandwich bag full of stones.

"And us too," Annie and Sam yelled, reaching in their backpacks to pull out their slingshots.

"Hold on there, mighty warriors," their father said laughing. "Let the police do their job, and we will save your slingshots for a last resort."

"Okay," the three younger children answered as they put their slingshots back in their bags.

They reached the police station and quickly found a place to park. The detective led them through the front door and into another door marked 'PRIVATE.' They walked down a narrow hallway passing several small offices on each side. At the end of the hallway, they went through another door into a large room bustling with activity.

There were a dozen or more desks scattered throughout the room. Only two of the people in the room were in police uniforms. All of the others were dressed like the detective they met at the boat landing or in normal everyday attire. Almost everyone in the room was talking on the phone.

"Come this way," the detective said, motioning for the family to follow him. "There's an empty conference room we can use over here."

He led them into a room located on the other side of the big room. The wall separating the two rooms was all glass. The children walked into the room and stood against the glass watching the activity in the other room.

"There's a pitcher of water and some cups in the corner," the detective told them. "I need to let the Sarge know you are here."

The detective gently closed the door and walked across the room. The children saw him walk to the desk of one of the uniformed policemen. He stood in front of the desk patiently waiting for the policeman to finish his phone call.

When he finally finished, the detective said something to him and pointed to the conference room. The uniformed man quickly grabbed a notebook and pen from his desk and headed toward the room.

The detective came through the door first and held the door open for the other gentleman.

"This is Sergeant Cooper," the detective said, "he is our supervisor and in charge of all ongoing investigations in our area."

"Please have a seat," he said as he put his notepad on the table. "My name is Sergeant Cooper, but around here everyone just calls me Sarge."

The children's father shook the Sergeant's hand and introduced himself. He then introduced the children's mother and each of the children from oldest to youngest.

After the introductions, everyone took a seat at the large table.

"I spoke with the detective by radio while you were traveling here. He tells me that we were not the only ones doing detective work on this case," the sergeant said smiling at the children.

Beth reached into her backpack and pulled out the memory card.

"We're hoping this will help with your investigation," she said.

The Sergeant reached across the table, taking the card from her. He then handed it to the detective.

"Take this to the lab," the Sergeant told the detective. "And tell those technicians I want some good facial pictures as quickly as possible."

After the detective left the room, the Sergeant leaned back in his chair. He gazed at the children, nodding his head while he gently rubbed his chin.

"Do you think you children could correctly identify those stolen vases if you saw them again?" Sarge asked.

"Absolutely," Mark said. "We made sketches of the vases and traced the drawings that were on the sides."

Beth pulled a notebook from her backpack and showed the drawings to the Sergeant.

"Excellent," Sarge said looking at the drawings.

"The drawings on the first ones we found were much more detailed than the one we found yesterday," Beth told the Sergeant.

"Wait a minute," the sergeant said smiling, "you mean to tell me you found another vase."

"Yes, sir," Beth answered.

"It's wrapped in tissue in a box in our vehicle," the children's mother said.

Everyone's attention was on the Sergeant. He sat there rubbing his chin again.

After a few moments of silence, he finally spoke.

"This is going to work perfectly," the sergeant said.

Suddenly there was a knock at the door. The detective who was with them earlier poked his head through the doorway.

"Sir," he said looking at the Sarge, "the gentleman from the Bureau of Indian Affairs is here."

"Show him in," the Sergeant told him.

The children immediately recognized their friend Mr. Hawkins and ran to the door to meet him. They all began talking at once, trying to explain to Mr. Hawkins everything that had happened since they last saw him.

"Slow down a little," their friend said laughing. "Let's have a seat, and you can tell me everything that has happened."

The Sergeant stood as Mr. Hawkins approached the table.

"I guess I'm the only one who needs an introduction," he said smiling.

They introduced themselves to each other and then took their seats at the table. After they were seated, the children told Mr. Hawkins all about their trap and the other artifacts they found.

"So, do we know what's on the film yet?" Mr. Hawkins asked.

"Not yet," the Sergeant answered, "but we should know before we're finished here."

"Finished with what?" Mr. Hawkins said curiously.

"Well," he began, "before you walked in, I was just about to ask these children if they would be interested in helping set another trap for the thieves. But of course," he added, "it would be with their parent's permission."

The children's attention turned to their parents, who were whispering to each other.

"As long as they are not in harm's way," the children's mother told the sergeant, "we will do whatever you ask to catch those thieves."

"Yes!" The children yelled, as the room filled with excitement.

CHAPTER TEN

It was almost noon by the time the Sergeant finished outlining his plan to catch the thieves. As he was finishing, a knock came at the door, and a young lady in a white lab coat entered.

"Sir," she said, smiling at everyone in the room, "those pictures you needed are ready."

"Great," he said, taking a large brown envelope from her hand.

The young lady politely excused herself and left the room.

The Sergeant went directly to the back wall of the room. Mounted to the wall was a large corkboard. He grabbed a box of tacks and began pulling out pictures and tacking them to the board.

As he was placing the last picture onto the board, he turned to everyone at the table.

"It seems there were two thieves," the sergeant said, finishing the pictures. "Would you like to take a look and see if your pizza man is in these pictures?" he asked.

Everyone eagerly went to the wall and began looking at the pictures.

"I don't see him," Mark said curiously.

"Isn't that him right there?" Timmy said with some doubt.

"No, it's not," Beth replied, pointing to a different photo. "This is a better picture of the same guy here."

"It looks like him, but it's definitely not," Mark said, looking at the picture.

"Well, who are they?" Beth asked.

"I don't know," the Sergeant said. "But I do know one thing, you children did a wonderful job. When we do find out who they are, it's going to be a closed case with these pictures."

"You sound pretty confident we're going to catch these guys," Mr. Hawkins said.

"If we can make our plan work," Sarge said smiling, "I think we'll flush these guys right out."

"Are we ready to get started?" Mr. Hawkins asked.

"Why don't you folks go grab a quick bite to eat while I get my detectives briefed," the Sergeant said.

"That sounds like a good plan," the children's mother said smiling.

"I am starting to get a little hungry," Annie said.

"But we are not doing pizza again," their father replied.

"Chinese buffet!" the children all yelled together.

Everyone began laughing out loud.

"I wish I could join you," Sarge said, "but we must meet back here at one o'clock sharp."

As expected, the children's father was thrilled about the choice to pick Chinese for lunch. Mr. Hawkins accepted their offer to join them. They chose a table at the far end of the restaurant where they could talk without being overheard.

Everyone was overwhelmed about the opportunity to help catch the thieves. While seated at the table, the children's mother had to ask several times for the children to lower their voices.

It was also the first time the children were given a chance to ask Mr. Hawkins about himself and the work that he did with the Bureau of Indian Affairs.

They were amazed to learn that he had grown up on an Indian reservation.

"What tribe of American Indians do you belong to?" Beth asked.

"I am a Chitimacha Indian," he told the children.

"That was one of the tribes you talked about that day at the point," Timmy said.

"You said that the name 'Chitimacha' meant 'the people of many waters,' and that they were skilled fishermen," Mark added.

"They were a tribe of many skills," he shared with them. "They were very good at producing crops and also great hunters. Hunting deer and buffalo in the winter helped to provide meat for their families, and they also used the hides from the animals to make clothing."

"They hunted buffalo in Louisiana?" Mark asked curiously.

"Yes," Big Joe answered. "Most people do not know that many years ago buffalo once roamed our land."

He explained to the children that the buffalo herds of the Great Plains of Texas and Oklahoma would travel on their winter migration across the Sabine River into the region. They would then travel to the south and east to find grazing lands because of the very mild winters. Many of the tribes of the southeast would hunt the buffalo to provide meat for their people.

The children were eager to learn about the American Indian tribes of their area, and Mr. Hawkins' was delighted to share with them his heritage.

He also told them what it was like growing up on the reservation. Since they did not have their own schools, he and the other children attended the local public school system in their area.

"It was very difficult in those days for the American Indian children," he told them.

"Were the other children mean to you all?" Annie asked.

"No, they were not mean. We just were not accepted. We were different, and I think that made others fearful of us. It is like that in most cases where people of a different culture must live among the masses."

"What about your culture made them the most fearful?" Beth asked.

"It was probably our connection to the land and all that it provided for us," Mr. Hawkins replied. "Our culture has a deep respect for the land. For centuries it provided everything we needed, and we were grateful for that. That connection to nature made others around us uncomfortable. Even though many of the American Indians worshiped the same God as everyone else and honored and served the same country, we were still seen as different because of our beliefs."

"Is it better today than it was then?" Mark asked.

"In most cases, it has gotten better," he answered. "But think about the reason I am sitting here with you today. The same people who once looked down on us are now stealing our heritage and selling it on black markets so they can use our history to decorate their homes."

"Wow," the children's mother said, "I didn't think about it that way."

"Sad, but true," Big Joe told her.

Mr. Hawkins continued telling the children about his life. After high school, he attended the state university and received a degree in criminal justice. A short time later, he went to work as a police officer. Within five years he worked his way into a detective's position.

"You were a detective?" Timmy exclaimed.

"For twenty years."

"How did you end up working with the Bureau of Indian Affairs?" Beth asked.

"I was in the right place at the right time," he said with a smile.

He told them that while working an investigation, he was required to travel to the nation's capital to interview a witness. While there, he met the national director of the Bureau and was asked to join them.

Knowing very little about the Bureau, he was amazed at the history that surrounded it. He explained to the children that the Bureau was originally called the Committee on Indian Affairs and created by Benjamin Franklin in 1775 with the help of the Continental Congress. The role of the committee at that time was to negotiate treaties and help the American Indians maintain their tribal communities. In 1824, the name was changed to the Bureau of Indian Affairs. Since then, the Bureau has worked with the government to represent all of the American Indian tribes, helping to preserve their culture.

Mr. Hawkins saw the opportunity to work for the Bureau of Indian Affairs as a way to help protect his heritage and still be involved in law enforcement.

"Do you enjoy what you do now?" Mark asked.

"Like police work, you are only called when there is a problem. But being able to correct those situations gives me a great feeling of accomplishment."

They continued visiting while enjoying their lunch. Mr. Hawkins told them about many of the cases he worked on and how the outcome of the cases created ways of doing things that protected the American Indian culture.

After they finished lunch, they drove back to the police station.

When they walked into the lobby of the station, they saw the Sergeant talking with a small group of people. Two of them were the detectives that had been investigating the thefts. Two others were policemen dressed in uniform. The last of the group, a middle-aged woman with red hair, listened as Sarge gave instructions. She was dressed in a dark blue dress with a broad white collar.

One of the detectives walked over to meet them. He took them back to the conference room where they had been before.

"Are you all ready to do some detective work?" the Sergeant said smiling, as he walked into the room with the lady that was with him in the lobby.

"Yes, sir," the children answered.

"Good," he replied. "I would like you to meet a very good friend of mine," he said, motioning to the lady. "This is detective Jane Jones with the State Police."

"It's a pleasure to meet you all," Ms. Jones said. "I have heard some wonderful things about you all."

"Thank you," the children said politely.

"Detective Jones is the reason we are all here today," he said. "Would you like to tell them exactly what you were able to uncover in your investigation?"

"Well," Ms. Jones began, "about three days ago we received a call from an art dealer in New Orleans. He said that he had been visited by a gentleman who was trying to appraise some pieces of Native American Indian pottery that he recently purchased. The art dealer was very suspicious of the man. He was able to get the location of the antique store where the pottery had been purchased but very little else."

"The pieces of pottery," the Sergeant added, "fit the description of a couple of the pieces you first discovered at your site."

"So, where is the antique store that sold the pieces?" Mr. Hawkins asked curiously.

"About thirty miles north of here, on Highway 1," he replied.

"And that is where I need your help," Ms. Jones said, smiling at the children.

"What can we do?" Beth asked.

"We need you to go to the antique store and see if you can positively identify any of the pieces that you discovered," she answered.

"We can do that," Mark said.

"Let me get with my officers, and I will let everyone know the plan," Sarge told them.

He returned a moment later with the two detectives and the two uniformed police officers.

"Listen up," the Sergeant said in a very serious tone. "I have a map for everyone with the location of the antique store. Detective Jones will leave first with the vase you children found yesterday. Everyone else will leave ten minutes behind her."

"When she arrives," he continued, "she will make contact with the owner and tell him she is interested in selling the vase."

"You folks," he said, pointing to the children and their parents, "should be arriving by then. You will proceed into the building and begin looking around. One of my plain clothes detectives will be right behind you. If you see anything that was stolen from the site, just make eye contact with him and simply nod your head. He will contact me and the other officers by radio. We will be stationed across the street. My two uniformed officers will be right down the highway waiting for my orders."

He paused for just a moment, looking at everyone.

"Are there any questions?" he asked.

"Is it really necessary for the three younger children to go into the store? Shouldn't we try to stay quiet and not draw attention to ourselves," Ms. Jones said.

"To be perfectly honest," the sergeant replied, "I have my concerns about that also. After all, we really don't know what we are walking in to," he added.

Timmy, Annie and Sam all lowered their heads in disappointment.

"I was kind of hoping you would let me cover the rear of the building in case anyone tried to make a run for it," Mr. Hawkins said as he winked at the Sergeant. "And I really could use some help with an important job like that. Of course, that would have to be with the permission of their parents."

"That would be just fine," the children's father said smiling.

"All right," Sarge said, "everyone be careful and keep your eyes open for any trouble."

Ms. Jones followed the family to their vehicle and took the box that contained the small vase.

"I will do my very best to keep whoever is there distracted while you look around," she told them.

"If there is anything in that store that came from our site, we will notice it," Beth replied confidently.

"I'm sure you will," Ms. Jones said, nodding her head.

She turned and walked to her car. Moments later she was driving away.

The children's mother saw Mr. Hawkins approaching them. She knelt in front of the three young children.

"I want the three of you to mind Mr. Hawkins," she said.

"Yes, ma'am."

"Is my help ready?" Mr. Hawkins said as he neared the group.

"I believe they are," the children's mother said.

"All we need is our backpacks, Boss," Timmy said, saluting his friend.

Annie and Sam began giggling.

"I hope you know what you've volunteered for," the children's father said laughing.

"I have five grandchildren all about their ages," he replied, "we are going to do just fine."

Timmy, Annie and Sam grabbed their backpacks from the truck and waited alongside Mr. Hawkins.

The children saw the Sergeant walking in their direction.

"Are we ready to roll?" he said, smiling at the group.

"I believe so," the children's father answered.

"My detective will enter the store right behind you," he assured them, "and we will be right across the street, ready to move in when he notifies us."

"Will he be packing heat?" Timmy said, crouching down and putting his hand out at his side like a gunfighter.

The Sergeant, who was trying to stay as serious as possible to make the family feel secure, burst into laughter.

"Yes," he said still laughing, "we will all be packing heat."

"He's a little excitable," Timmy's mother said, pulling him close to her. "I'm sure everything's going to be just fine."

"I'm sure it will too," Sarge said, still chuckling.

Within minutes, the caravan of automobiles rolled onto the highway, heading north to their destination.

CHAPTER ELEVEN

Beth and Mark watched out the back window as the cars followed them down the road.

The two cars directly behind them had no markings on them. The first was driven by the detective who was going to follow them into the store. The second had the Sergeant and the other detective who was working the case with them. Behind that car, Mr. Hawkins trailed with their younger brothers and sister.

Beth and Mark also noticed in the distance a regular police car, which was supposed to be carrying the two uniformed policemen.

"Are you nervous?" Mark asked Beth.

"I'm not sure if it's nerves," she replied, "but my hands are shaking."

"Maybe it is just excitement," Mark said, "because I'm a little shaky too."

"Yeah," Beth agreed, nodding her head, "that must be what it is."

****

Three cars back, however, the situation was quite different. Timmy was ready for action, and his two sidekicks were ready to follow.

"This is our first real detective job," Timmy said boldly, "so if you see us doing anything wrong, just let us know."

"That's right," Annie and Sam said quickly, agreeing with their brother.

"I'm sure you're going to do just fine," Mr. Hawkins replied with a smile. "But if I see anything, I will let you know."

"We should have everything we need," Timmy said, as the three of them began digging in their backpacks.

"We all brought our slingshots and I brought a big bag of really good shooting rocks," Timmy said, as he shook the bag of rocks for Mr. Hawkins to hear. "We each brought a banana, too," he added, "but since we only have three, we will each give you a piece of ours if we get hungry."

"That will be just fine," Mr. Hawkins said laughing.

"And I brought my binoculars, a whistle and a bag with some rubber bands," Annie said proudly.

"And I brought my magnifying glass, a piece of rope and a bag with some feathers," Sam said, not intending to be left out of the conversation.

"I can't think of anything else we might need," Mr. Hawkins said, as he continued driving. "I think we are good to go."

****

With good weather and very little midday traffic, the trip did not take long.

"According to the map," Beth told her father, "the antique store should be just ahead on the right-hand side."

"There it is," Mark pointed out. "And there is Detective Jones' car."

"Let's just stay calm and remember why we're here," the children's mother said, taking a deep breath.

"Are you nervous, Mom?" Beth asked.

"No, of course not," she said laughing. "We are about to walk into this building and help the police catch a couple thieves. It's just another adventure, right?"

"It will be just fine," her husband assured her.

After parking, Beth, Mark and their parents exited the vehicle. Beth noticed Mr. Hawkins' vehicle going behind a small feed and hardware store that was located next door.

The antique store seemed to be a bit of an antique itself. The old wood-framed building, set off the ground on small concrete blocks, had a large porch that ran across the entire front of the structure. The outside of the building, with its rusty tin roof, had once been

painted red, but very little of the color could still be seen on the weathered wood planks. Above the aged wooden steps that went up to the porch, a sign hung on two rusty pieces of chain. Painted in gold was the single word 'ANTIQUES.'

As they walked up the steps and prepared to enter the building, the two children noticed the detective parking his car in the parking lot next to their vehicle. Mark noticed that he was wearing a sports coat, which covered the embroidered Sheriff's badge on the front of his shirt.

The two children turned and entered through the front door of the antique store, followed by their mother and father. Beth and Mark were amazed at the size of the interior of the building.

Paintings and old pictures covered the front wall from floor to ceiling. All the way along the left wall were open shelves, filled with knickknacks and collectibles. On the opposite side of the room, large cabinets with glass fronts lined the wall. It appeared that was where the more expensive things were located. In the center of the room were rows of antique tables, chairs and other types of furniture.

The back wall, covered with more pictures and paintings, also housed a large collection of clocks. In each corner were large double doors that appeared to lead to a storage area in the rear of the building. Near the center of the back wall was a huge wooden desk with brass floor lamps on each side. Seated at the desk were two people.

Although Detective Jones was seated with her back to them, the children knew it was her because of her blue dress. The gentleman she was talking with at the desk looked very familiar to Beth and Mark.

"I think we should start over there," the children's mother said, putting her hands on their shoulders and steering them to the wall with the glass cases.

"Dad, I think that is one of the men from the pictures," Mark whispered.

"It may be," their father said, "but we are here to identify stolen property. And that needs to be our focus."

As they proceeded along the wall, looking at each case carefully, they could hear Detective Jones talking about the vase and trying to get the gentleman to give her a value on it.

They heard the front door squeak and turned to see the detective entering the store. He gave them a quick glance and then began walking toward the opposite wall.

Beth and Mark made their way through the aisle studying each shelf in the glass cabinets. Old glass vases and dishes covered most of the shelves. As they continued along the wall Mark turned to Beth and whispered.

"If we were to come to a place like this on any other day, we would be so excited to see all of this stuff."

"I know," Beth replied, trying to smile.

****

Mr. Hawkins drove his vehicle around the rear of the antique store. Behind the store were two old flatbed trailers and an old shed that appeared to be abandoned. He parked just behind the old shed. From that location, they had a clear view of the building.

"When I was working as a detective, we always made sure the rear of a location was covered on a job like this," Mr. Hawkins told them.

"I'm glad we have someone with your experience backing us up," Timmy told him.

Mr. Hawkins chuckled at Timmy's comment.

"So, what do we do now?" Annie asked.

"We wait," he answered.

****

Beth and Mark were just over halfway down the aisle when they notice something familiar. They dropped to their knees with their hands and faces against the glass.

"That's one of our vases," Beth whispered excitedly.

"It is," Mark quickly confirmed.

"Are you sure?" their father asked.

"Yes sir, absolutely," she replied. "That is the vase that was broken. You can see where they glued the piece that was broken back onto the top."

Mark reached into his pocket and unfolded the sketch they made at the site while she was talking.

"Dad, that is definitely it," Mark responded, holding the picture against the glass and comparing them.

Their father looked across the room to get the attention of the detective. When the detective finally looked their way, their father nodded his head.

Beth and Mark stood to see the detective pull a small radio from his coat pocket and talk into it. He then started walking to the desk where the gentleman and Ms. Jones were seated.

When he was a few steps from the desk, he pulled out his badge and held it in the air.

"Could I have a few moments of your time?" the detective said in a loud voice.

Detective Jones immediately stood and pulled her badge from her purse.

"We would like to talk to you about some stolen property in your store," she told the gentleman.

Just then the front doors burst open and in came the Sergeant and the other detective.

As they made their way to the center of the room toward the desk, Beth noticed the rear door closest to them slowly opening. She saw a face emerge from the opening that she immediately recognized.

"Dad, it's the waiter from the pizza parlor," she yelled.

The slamming door caught the attention of the Sergeant and the detective.

"Check it out!" the Sergeant yelled, as he pointed to the door.

The detective ran to the door. With his right hand stuck in his coat, he stopped and put his ear to the door.

****

Timmy, Annie and Sam sat in the back seat of Mr. Hawkins' car, closely watching the rear of the building.

"Look!" Annie yelled. "Someone is trying to open that window!"

"We have to get closer," Timmy said, grabbing his slingshot.

"Wait," Mr. Hawkins said, "I'm supposed to keep the three of you away from trouble, remember."

"But we can't let him get away," Timmy pleaded.

"Okay," Mr. Hawkins said, "but you all need to stay close to me."

The three children, with slingshots in hand, made their way toward the building with Mr. Hawkins leading them.

****

The detective was standing motionless, with his ear still to the door.

Suddenly from the back room came the sound of breaking glass.

"Ouch! Stop that!" someone yelled. "Don't do that! Ouch! Stop!" they yelled again.

The detective pushed open the door and ran into the room.

They heard the sound of glass breaking again.

"Stop that! OUCH! Would someone please help me!"

Beth and Mark felt their mother's hands on their shoulders as she pulled them in close to her.

It suddenly became very quiet.

Moments later the detective came through the door laughing and shaking his head.

"The situation is under control," he told Sarge.

"What do you mean?"

"See for yourself," the detective said, pointing to the front door.

After several seconds, Mr. Hawkins came walking through the front door, holding the waiter from the pizza parlor by the back of his collar. And right behind him, with slingshots in hand, marched the three proudest junior detectives anyone had ever seen.

"We caught this one trying to sneak out the back window," Mr. Hawkins said.

"Those crazy kids," Mr. Hawkins' captive said, "I'm going to have a bump the size of a golf ball on my head because of them and their slingshots, not to mention all the other bruises."

The Sergeant walked face to face with the young gentleman that Mr. Hawkins was holding.

"I think by the end of the day that will be the least of your worries," he told him.

"I don't know what this is all about," the gentleman behind the desk said. "If there is stolen property in this store, maybe I purchased it from someone else," he added.

"I don't think so," the Sergeant said, pulling a picture from his pocket and placing it on the desk.

The man studied the picture of himself with a flashlight and a shovel, walking through the site at Willow Hammock.

"It was a trap?" the gentleman behind the desk said with a puzzled look.

"I'm afraid so," the sergeant said smiling.

"So, the little vase with a gold coin in it was part of the trap," the waiter from the pizza parlor said.

The Sergeant looked over at Mark and Beth.

The two children shrugged their shoulders and shook their heads no.

"I guess not," Sarge responded, "but I would suggest you turn it over to us."

The gentleman at the desk grunted.

"We are in enough trouble already, little brother," he scowled, "maybe you should be quiet."

"Sorry," the younger gentleman said.

"Read them their rights and get them to the station," the Sergeant told the detectives.

"Yes, sir," they responded, as they led their two captives out the front door.

Sarge walked over to where Mr. Hawkins was standing.

"So, you actually let these kids open fire on my suspect with slingshots while he was trying to escape," he whispered in Mr. Hawkins' ear.

"Well," he replied smiling, "when I saw that he wasn't carrying any kind of weapon, I thought to myself, 'This might be fun to watch.'"

The two men laughed for a moment before returning to the others.

"It will probably take us weeks to figure out what is stolen in this place and what is not," Detective Jones said.

"But when it's all done, we will have these folks to thank," Sarge said, pointing to the children and their parents.

"I'm glad we were able to help," their father said.

"And I, too, will be forever grateful," Mr. Hawkins said. "And I will never forget," he continued, as he knelt in front of the three youngest children, "how bravely the three of you acted today."

Timmy, Annie and Sam beamed with pride as Mr. Hawkins gave them each a hug.

The Sergeant thanked them again as they made their way onto the front porch of the antique store.

"I'm sure you all will be hearing from us in a few days," he told them.

"It will probably take me that long to get the children's heads out of the clouds," their mother said.

Everyone said their farewells and headed in their own direction.

Timmy avoided the steps off the porch and jumped onto the grass and dirt. And, of course, his two sidekicks, Annie and Sam, followed right behind him.

Beth, Mark and their parents follow the three warriors across the parking lot.

"Let me tell you," Timmy said to Annie and Sam, "that dude didn't stand a chance with us and our slingshots."

"Not a chance," Annie added.

"I popped him right in the head," Sam said, closing one eye and acting like he was shooting again.

"It's a good thing Mr. Hawkins grabbed him when he did," Timmy boasted, "or I would've popped him right between the eyes."

"Me too," Annie said.

"And me too," Sam added.

Beth put her arm on Mark's shoulder.

"Oh, Brother! Here we go again," she said, as they burst into laughter.

CHAPTER TWELVE

It was very difficult for the children to get back on a regular schedule for the next few days. Every free moment, every school break, and every meal were filled with conversations about their adventure.

They heard the story of how the three youngest and Mr. Hawkins managed to sneak up on the gentleman crawling out of the window at least a dozen times.

The day after their return to Willow Hammock, the entire family took a trip to the shell point at the river to check the condition of the washout. They were pleased to see that the tides had not damaged the site since their last trip there.

To make sure that no further damage would be done, their father brought two shovels and several buckets with them to make a dam across the opening.

Using shells from the larger reef at the river's edge, they were able to close the opening and hopefully stop any further damage from the tides.

They decided not to search the site for more artifacts until they heard from Mr. Hawkins.

On the third day after the capture of the thieves, their father cooked a chicken and sausage gumbo and invited Mr. Jacobs to join them at the houseboat for supper. The children enjoyed telling him the details of their great adventure. He especially enjoyed Timmy telling him about the capture of the young man crawling out of the window. He was also pleased to hear that his dear friend Mr. Hawkins was able to help with the recovery of the stolen artifacts.

The following day, the excitement started all over again.

It was just before lunch when the children saw Deputy Cook's boat approaching the houseboat.

The children asked their mother if it was all right for them to stop their schoolwork to go meet him. She agreed, and the children bolted out of the houseboat to see Deputy Cook.

They were pleasantly surprised to see Sergeant Cooper and Mr. Hawkins with him. The children's parents joined them at the dock just as the deputy's boat arrived.

"Ahoy there," Sarge yelled with a big grin on his face.

"Ahoy," the children yelled back.

They tied the boat to the dock and exchanged greetings with everyone.

"How about I put on a pot of coffee, and everyone can come inside," the children's mother said.

"That would be great," they all agreed.

After everyone was inside and comfortably seated, the sergeant began telling them the details of their investigation.

He told them that the two thieves caught at the store were brothers. That was why the thief in the pictures looked familiar. The second gentleman in the pictures was an employee of the brother. He was caught later the same day by one of Ms. Jones' detectives trying to sell some stolen property in New Orleans.

The Sergeant also told them that he and his men had already found stolen items from eight reported thefts in the antique store.

"Are they all still in your jail?" Mark asked after he finished talking.

"Oh, yes," he answered, "and they will be in jail for quite some time."

"The people at the Bureau of Indian Affairs would like me to extend a thank you to all of you for helping to catch these men," Mr. Hawkins said.

"And there is one more piece of business they would like me to discuss with you," Mr. Hawkins added. "Since the artifacts found were on your property, we would like to get your permission to put the artifacts into our museums and visitor centers to help teach others about our heritage and customs."

"I think I speak for everyone when I say that would be wonderful," the children's father said.

"I also have a request from the State University," Mr. Hawkins told them. "They were amazed at the condition of the vases and artifacts that you found and would like to have your permission to do more research."

"Wow," Mark said. "We would have a real research team working here?"

"That's right," Mr. Hawkins said. "But we do have one problem with that."

"What's the problem?" Beth asked.

"Whenever the university sends a research team into the field, they prefer to find locals who are familiar with the area to help guide them and keep them safe. We would have to find a group that would be willing to work with them."

"That could be our job!" Timmy yelled excitedly.

"Well," Mr. Hawkins said with a smile, "with your mother and father's permission, we can make this happen."

The children looked at their parents.

"It was your find," their mother told them.

"And there is no one else that knows the area and the things to watch out for better than you all," their father added.

"So, we can lead the research team," Beth said.

"Sure," their mother said, "it sounds like a great class project to me."

"Yes!" they yelled.

"I will place the call as soon as we get in and see if we can do it as soon as possible," Mr. Hawkins responded.

The children's mother poured all of the adults a cup of coffee as everyone continued to visit.

Their father and mother visited with Mr. Hawkins and Sarge while the children told Deputy Cook the story of their adventure all over again.

As the conversation began to come to an end and everyone was preparing to say goodbye, the sergeant suddenly stood up.

"I can't believe I almost forgot to tell you," Sarge exclaimed.

The children filled with excitement again.

"Tell us what?" they all said.

"Well, it seems," he continued, "that the thieves did find a gold coin that night, buried in one of the vases that they recovered."

"Are you serious?" Beth said.

"So, I called Mr. Hawkins to tell him of our findings," Sarge said. "Mr. Hawkins, would you like to tell them what you found out?"

"After getting a description of the coin," Mr. Hawkins told them, "I called a good friend of mine in the Florida Keys who has a similar job as mine. I explained to him the situation and sent him a picture of the coin. He returned my call the following day after doing a bit of investigating and finding out that the coin was actually a Portuguese gold coin. After doing a little more research, he explained that during the period in which these tribes would have lived near your point, the Portuguese did not use the river for trade. It was mostly French, Spanish and English. It was his conclusion that the coin must have arrived in this area due to pirate activity."

"Whoa," Timmy exclaimed, "we had pirates right here on our land."

"It appears so," Mr. Hawkins said. "They probably did trade with the local Indians."

"That's awesome," Beth said.

"That's not all the good news," the sergeant continued. "The Bureau of Indian Affairs did not consider this a true American Indian artifact, so they agreed that it must be returned to its rightful owners. In this instance, it is the landowners.

He reached into his pocket, pulled out a large gold coin, and flipped it in the air to Beth. She caught it and placed it in the palm of her hand. The other children gathered around her and stared at the coin.

"Wow," Mark said with amazement.

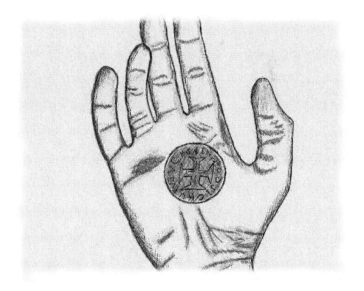

"There were real pirates right here on our land," Timmy yelled.

"It appears so," Beth said, as she flipped the coin over for everyone to view the other side.

"And if there were pirates, there were pirate ships," Mark stated confidently.

"And if there were pirate ships, there are probably more of these out there somewhere," Timmy added.

Beth looked up at her brothers and sister with a twinkle in her eyes.

"It sounds like we may have another adventure on our hands," she said.

THE END

About the Author

C. P. Landry is a lifelong resident of South Louisiana and a descendent of the original French Acadians now known as Cajuns. His wife of 40 years shares a similar heritage as the fifth generation to hunt, trap, and fish the marshes of the Atchafalaya River Basin. Together, they raised their five children to respect both their heritage and their land. The Cajun Kids Adventures Series is loosely based on the experiences, challenges and shenanigans of his children's unique upbringing.

More Adventures

Coming Soon!

Connect With Us!

f ◎ 𝓟

@cajunkidsadventures

info@cajunkids.com

www.cajunkids.com